TORNADO
on HORSEBACK

Also by Nelson Nye
in Large Print:

The Clifton Contract
Come A-Smokin'
Strawberry Roan
Desert of the Damned
Gringo
Gun-Hunt for the Sundance Kid
The Last Bullet
Shotgun Law
The Texas Gun
Gunfight at the O.K. Corral
Gunshot Trail
The Overlanders
Quick-Trigger Country
Ranger's Revenge
The Seven Six-Gunners

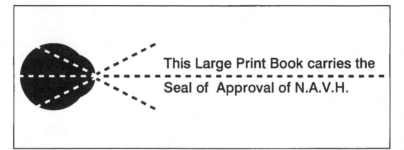

This Large Print Book carries the
Seal of Approval of N.A.V.H.

TORNADO
on HORSEBACK

Original Title: Fiddle-Back Ranch

NELSON NYE

Thorndike Press   **Waterville, Maine**

Published in 2003 by arrangement with Golden West Literary Agency.

Thorndike Press® Large Print Paperback Series.

The tree indicium is a trademark of Thorndike Press.

The text of this Large Print edition is unabridged. Other aspects of the book may vary from the original edition.

Set in 16 pt. Plantin by Minnie B. Raven.

Printed in the United States on permanent paper.

Library of Congress Cataloging-in-Publication Data

Nye, Nelson C. (Nelson Coral), 1907–
    [Fiddle-back ranch]
    Tornado on horseback / Nelson Nye.
      p. cm.
    ISBN 0-7862-5504-8 (lg. print : sc : alk. paper)
    1. Ranch life — Fiction.   2. Large type books.   I. Title.
PS3527.Y33F53 2003
  813'.54—dc21   2003048367

For
CHARLIE
of the Half Circle W

As the Founder/CEO of NAVH, the only national health agency solely devoted to those who, although not totally blind, have an eye disease which could lead to serious visual impairment, I am pleased to recognize Thorndike Press as one of the leading publishers in the large print field.

Founded in 1954 in San Francisco to prepare large print textbooks for partially seeing children, NAVH became the pioneer and standard setting agency in the preparation of large type.

Today, those publishers who meet our standards carry the prestigious "Seal of Approval" indicating high quality large print. We are delighted that Thorndike Press is one of the publishers whose titles meet these standards. We are also pleased to recognize the significant contribution Thorndike Press is making in this important and growing field.

Lorraine H. Marchi, L.H.D.
Founder/CEO
NAVH

1. The Girl at Single Cinch

Mark Connifay looked across his shoulder for the hundredth time. Futilely, one would have said, for his trail across those furnace-hot flats loomed desolate in every particular. Yet one would have been mistaken if one had assumed that Mark's backward staring was of little import. Connifay had reached a bitter conclusion, the culmination of these many glances and long hours of deliberate thought: *No man could run from himself, or leave his destiny behind.*

Man was born to that which Fate had mapped for him; no other course was possible, no other career attainable. This bitter conviction was the sole fruit gleaned by him from twenty-four years of living.

He had started well enough; a prosperous rancher's son with a leaning toward the creature comforts. But he had not known such comforts long. A cattle feud over in Texas had years back put the Old Man's name on a headstone, leaving Mark — the last of the Connifays — to carve his own trail from Smith's Crossing. He had carved it, too, but had found in the achievement very little he could take real pride in.

Yet he'd got along well enough till some unsuspected soft streak deep within him had taken him back to Smith's Crossing. His wide lips curled as he thought of it. A thing for suckers — sentiment; he hoped he'd have the wit to remember it. He'd quit the Crossing between dark and dawn, and hadn't much cared whose horse he took, either.

He sighed and then, with an impatient jerk of his big scarred hands, he caught up the reins; kneed the tired horse on.

It seemed as if the feud which had finished Mark's boyhood had left a few coals in the ashes. These, with the Law's tin pinned to their shirtfronts, had been camping right hard ever since on Mark's backtrail; but he guessed he'd shaken them finally. There had been no sign of their dust for two days.

Single Cinch was a spavined place on the rump of the Organ Mountains, an adobe eruption just an easy shot west of the break where the grim San Andreas joined with the Organs to present a hundred-mile barrier to caravans east and west-bound across the country's wastelands. This was a wild new Territory, and Single Cinch was hardly more than a stage stop on the threadlike trail that, spanning these terrible distances, connected faroff Roswell with equally faroff Silver.

As a town Single Cinch had not even the periodic value of a shipping point, for no railroad came within miles of it. Yet it had its use. As an escape valve for such hardy souls as had ventured to root in this country, it was a rendezvous of the tallest order.

The Valley outfits usually took it in turn; these turns being watchfully managed so that only one outfit came in at a time. It was safest thus, and the merchants approved it, for life and the sanctity of private property were things held cheaply by these turbulent riders. Other times, reps for these spreads only raised the town's dust upon such occasions as the ordering of supplies made a visit a reluctant necessity. Such was Single Cinch, attracting few who dared go elsewhere.

It was eight o'clock of a close, still evening when a stranger stepped into the Cap and Ball. He was a tall man, lean, wind-whipped and dusty; dark, with a high-boned, rugged face strangely at variance with his black frock coat, string tie and white linen. A gambling man, you would have said from his look, yet there were things about him not wholly compatible with that diagnosis. The frock coat sat too tight on his shoulders and his stride told of much time spent in the saddle. Not even his hands looked wholly right; quick and long-fingered but too big — callus-roughened. And his face was too bronzed. It showed a fighter's features, high, flat and stubborn, but the eyes were a gambler's eyes. Cool, inscrutable, perfectly masking his thoughts.

He stopped by the door with his eyes narrowed watchfully, afterwards approaching the bar with a cool, free stride. He had a small drink and took a look round the room, his glance lingering longest on a man with his chair tilted back to the wall. The man in the chair gave no sign of noticing. With his eyes kept fast on the ceiling, he worried an off-key melody.

"Been a long time since I heard that tune," the man in the frock coat said reflectively. "They give a different twist to it . . . there."

But nobody asked him where that was; and after a moment he took a cigar from his pocket and calmly lit it while his cool glance studied the man in the chair.

"Any gent in these parts need a ridin' man?"

A queer little silence followed the question. Then the barman said, "Don't hardly seem likely, unless —" He shot a quick look at the man in the chair. "Unless Vidal Shain could make out to use you."

"Shain?"

"Runs the Lazy S — that's him in the chair."

A darkened look edged the stranger's stare. "What's the matter with him — deaf?"

Shain quit his humming. "Are you talkin' at me?"

"Have you got any ridin' jobs empty?"

"Who's wantin' one — you?"

The stranger's cigar rolled across flat lips. A trace of blue smoke trickled out through his teeth. They were white and hard and strong, those teeth, and, just now, rather wicked.

He said no words, but Shain's glance fell. He pulled out his cheeks and his lips curled wryly. "Guess not," he said, and returned to his humming.

The gambler's eyes turned black as jet and the tip of his smoke got suddenly red and he was lifting his elbows off the bar when a girl's sharp cry rang out above them.

It came from a room off the balcony. Shearing frantically across that sudden hush, it brought the gambler, eyes glinting, away from the bar. His glance flashed up, then down again, swiftly, to observe what change might have crossed Shain's features.

The stillness deepened, grew tighter and tighter. Outside, a risen wind whistled on the eaves; and overhead a struggle lashed sound through the building.

There came a sudden curse — the crash of a door. A girl showed above them, disheveled and frantic as she made for the stairhead. A mustached man sprang after her, cursing.

The girl screamed again as the man caught her shoulders.

The gambler's boots took him up the stairs as the legs of Shain's chair struck the floor with a clatter. Shain yelled. "Damn you, Bannock!"

But the mustached man had a firm hold on the girl again. He was pantingly dragging her back toward the room when he saw the gambler step onto the balcony.

A paralysis froze him. He went utterly still.

The gambler said: "Let go of her, Bannock."

Bannock's cheeks were gray. They went tight with hate and he snatched for his pistol, but the gambler's fist took him full in the face, smashing him backward. Bannock's clutch missed the rail and, with arms flailing wildly, he went down the stairs.

When he came to his senses the gambler stood over him.

"Get up on your feet."

"By Gawd!" Bannock shouted; but the hand he drove hipward found his gun leather empty. He stood trapped, his face twisted, his bloated lips snarling. He grabbed for a knife he had cached in his collar.

It was all the excuse the gambler needed. He took one forward step and struck.

Bannock went down like a pole-axed steer.

The girl came down the stairs slowly. There were strange bright glints in her dark, full stare, and she seemed even yet unable to credit such swift disaster as had overtaken Bannock. She adjusted her clothing, watching the stranger with an odd, intent interest.

Perhaps she was piqued that he did not look at her. A darker light ran through her eyes and the painted lines of her lips altered subtly. Then the man looked up and her whole face changed. She dropped her glance shyly, and when it lifted the look of her was wholly sober. She said, "I'm Bella Mae Brady, an' mighty obliged —"

"You better get out of here," the gambler told her. "Better get out now before this polecat recovers."

He had no look for her; his gaze stayed on Bannock. But after a moment she smiled, rather tightly, shook out her red curls and stopped by the banister.

The resettled stillness was finally broken by the man on the floor. Bannock groaned — groaned again, and came groggily up on an unsteady elbow. You could tell by his start when remembrance hit him.

He did not jump up nor waste breath cursing. Caution was mingled with his passions now. There was blood on his mouth and he wiped it off.

He got up finally, watchfully, carefully.

The gambler said, "Get your hat, Bannock."

Bannock picked up his hat.

A wildness threaded the room and was felt. The mustached Bannock shook his shoulders together. He touched his bruised jaw with a shaking hand.

"Get your gun."

Bannock glared. Malevolence grated in the rasp of his breathing.

Black hate was a light in the man's glinting stare. Violence was in him, tugging him, jerking him. Violence and hatred and a plain will to murder.

Then he grinned with his teeth and crossed to the stairs and, close by the girl, bent and picked up his pistol.

The room went so still men could hear their hearts beating. But Bannock seemed to know that this wasn't his night. He dropped the gun in his holster and shoved through the batwings.

They heard him leave town at a headlong gallop.

2. Timpas

No one said anything for several moments; then the bar-man grinned. "Bejasus, *that* was tellin' him!"

The gambler's glance found the redhead watching him. Her eyes were smiling and her cheeks held excitement. By the look of her blouse she had little on under it. Her skirt was too short and too tight at the hips — probably too tight purposely. He knew her trade and had no quarrel with it; she served a useful purpose in this country, like gamblers and cappers and the rest of the riffraff.

His eyes showed a bitter contempt for himself; but they also warned that the contempt was his. Others could show similar scorn at their own grim risk.

Restlessness swayed the girl. She brought her arms up over her breasts and swept back her hair with long, slim fingers. She smiled at him frankly; and he suddenly turned and would have crossed the room to her except that the house man, Dorado Stoggins, chose that moment to get up and approach him.

Stoggins said, "Perhaps, if you're looking for work, I could —"

The man's cold eyes looked through him frostily. Stoggins' glance, like his words, trailed off unfinished. He turned with a flush and went back to his card game.

The stranger puffed his cigar back to life and through its smoke eyed the bold, free swing of the girl's comely body. She was watching him again, and her dark eyes glinted. She sat down at a table underneath the balcony; and when he came over she laughed at him softly.

"You're no gambler," she said.

"No?"

"Of course not — only a cowboy would use his fists."

He said nothing to that; and before she could speak again Shain came over and stood with the flats of his fists on the table. He grinned, and something secret looked out of his stare. "About that job," he said meaningly. "I've changed my mind —"

The gambler said: "I don't like people who change their minds."

Shain stared, kind of scowled and then shrugged indifferently. "I just wanted to say —"

"Yeah; I know. I'll remember."

Vidal Shain's lips pulled away from his

17

teeth and he quit the place without further talk, the sound of his boots drifting hollowly back.

Taking the cigar from his mouth, the gambler eyed it somberly. "In every community," he said, speaking thoughtfully, "there's always a boss."

"You're wantin' to know who's bossing this one?"

He turned the cigar around in his fingers. "I can always find out."

"Look," she said, leaning forward abruptly. "Keep out of this, mister."

He smiled at her thinly.

The swell of her breasts stirred gently and she said, "Play it smart. Get on your horse and get out of here, Connifay."

"So you know me, do you?"

"I know Bannock. A bad lot. Shoves folks around like he's cock of the walk; but I saw his face when you came up those stairs. Reminded me of something. He came from Smith's Crossing. There was quite a fight over there two-three years ago. Bannock cut and run for it along with some other toughs. . . . A man named Connifay proved tougher than they were."

They regarded each other very thoughtfully then.

"Think he recognized me, do you?"

She put a hand on his arm. "Listen. That's the first time I ever saw Bannock get backed up. He's made a name in this country — an ugly name, granted — but do you suppose —"

"Mmmm, I see your point," nodded Connifay. He got up, chucking his cigar toward the gleam of a cuspidor. "Much obliged f—"

"Hello, Bella Mae. Who's your friend?" said a new voice.

Connifay turned in mild irritation.

He saw the man near them, urbanely smiling. Big and well dressed in an expensive garb of a new Eastern cut. An emerald, worn on a middle finger, was precisely the shade of his sleep-lidded eyes. He looked suave and polished, and the only thing Western about his appearance was the huge white Stetson which he held in his hand.

The girl said, "Ely, this is Mark Connifay. Mark, shake hands with Ely Timpas, buggy boss of the Wet Moon syndicate. If you're hunting a job he can probably use you; if things break right he's going to be our next governor."

"There, there," Timpas smiled, "let's not start counting chickens." He nodded to Connifay. "Glad to know you," he said.

"Any friend of Miss Brady can be counted a friend of mine." He looked Connifay over. "A stranger, I take it. Are you trying to find work?"

Connifay saw the girl's look and took a perverse pleasure in ignoring it. He said, "That all depends," and bit the end off a fresh cigar.

"I could probably make a place for you. Any good at figures?"

Connifay said with a wry kind of smile, "I'm out here for my health, Mr. Timpas. The doctor advised open air and sunshine."

Timpas' lip did not curl. "That could be arranged, I guess. We hire a good many hands. Ever work on a ranch?"

"I expect I could make out to stay on a horse."

Timpas inspected him casually. "Use a gun, can you?"

"I've shot a few rounds at targets."

"We've been losing a lot of cattle lately. Might be that brushwood gang that came in here last year. If I put you on as strayman you might be able to learn something for us."

He looked across at the house man. "Where's that barman of yours, Dorado?"

"Getting thirsty, Guv'nor?"

"Guess we could all do with a small one. Pretty close out tonight."

"We could do with some rain," Stoggins said. "What'll you have, Guv'nor?"

"Wait — I'll fix it," Bella Mae said, rising. She went back of the bar. Timpas' admiring glance following her.

Connifay said, "Range pretty dry, is it?"

"*We've* got water — or we'll have plenty shortly. We're taking over a couple more outfits on the first of the month. Once we get Kroniac's —"

"That's the Fiddle-Back, ain't it?"

Timpas' glance came round sharply.

"Fella I met on the trail said he was needin' hands."

Timpas' smile was clipped. "He was funning you — Kroniac's hands ain't been paid in six months. Never *will* get their money unless I take care of them. Fiddle-Back's one of the outfits I'm taking over. Old man's stone broke —"

"And prouder than sheep dip!" Bella Mae said.

The big man chuckled, looking across at her knowingly. "Yes, he's proud — they all are, for that matter. Still livin' in the days when they bossed this valley." Timpas' shrug dismissed them. "By the way," he said casually, "aren't you from Texas?"

Connifay smiled. "I didn't say."

Lamplight gleamed in Bella Mae's copper hair. "Come an' get it," she called.

Timpas, setting down his glass, smacked his lips. "Best drink I've had since I left El Paso!" He smiled at the girl. Then, pulling up his glance, he looked at Connifay. "So you're wanting work, eh?"

"He's too sick to work," Bella Mae said quickly; and Stoggins, the house man, leered across his whisky. Bella Mae ignored him. "He's on his way to Denver. Going to take some kind of treatment —"

"Him?" Timpas stared, forgetting his manners. "If I had *his* physique —"

"Oh, but you don't know! You haven't seen him cough! Why, he's just like a wrung-out dishrag." Over Timpas' shoulder her eyes frowned a warning.

But Connifay said: "I do pretty fair; I'm picking up fast. Been keepin' outdoors —"

Timpas, eying the healthy bronze of his cheeks, said: "I can well believe it." He stared for a moment longer. "Tell you what I'll do," he said then. "You come along out to the Wet Moon and I'll put you on as strayman —"

Bella Mae said sharply: "He's a sick man, Ely. If you're bound and determined to help him, buy him a ticket to Denver and get him some place he can use it."

"Well . . ." Timpas said, and looked at her curiously.

Connifay's shrug deprecated her words. For some obscure reason she didn't want the Wet Moon boss to hire him. Why Timpas should be *wanting* to hire him was the thing that intrigued Mark Connifay. What had he stumbled onto here? Of what kind of use could a gambler be to a fellow like Timpas — on a cow ranch?

He asked: "How much could I earn with you, Timpas?"

It pulled Timpas' glance back reluctantly. But he got his smile working and said with some show of heartiness, "I couldn't start you off better than one-twenty. However, if you work out as well as I think you will, I expect we could pay a few bonuses."

Connifay looked at him. "Bonuses, eh?"

Bella Mae flounced away from the bar, grabbed up her glass and went off to a table.

"From time to time," Timpas said easily, "we ought to be able to work a few extras in."

"Ah . . . this one-twenty you mentioned. That would be a dollar and twenty cents a day, I suppose —"

"A hundred and twenty a month," Timpas said; and Connifay looked at him tightly.

The edge of his glance got very bright. "So it's *that* kind of job! Well, the answer's *no!* You better go talk to a gun fighter, Timpas —"

"I am," Timpas said.

3. "Shooting's Too Good for You!"

"You sure played hell!" a voice at his elbow accused him as Connifay was saddling his horse the next morning.

He knew without turning it was Bella Mae talking, and he knew without turning she was downright angry. It sounded as if she wanted to break something; he knew without looking what her eyes would have shown him.

"Never mind," he said, going on with his saddling. "It's my neck I'm risking, an' I've risked it before. I know what I'm doing."

She said hotly: "I doubt it! Ely Timpas is no man to trifle with; no one but a *fool* would fuss him up that way. Why did you do it? Why did you egg him on when I had it all fixed —"

"Mebbe," he said, "I didn't want it fixed that way."

"Mebbe," she mimicked, "you'd rather find yourself *planted!*"

"I can take care of that, too."

"You fool!" she flamed. "Do you think you can laugh at a man like Timpas and not be called to account for it?"

Connifay shrugged, yanked the flank girth tight and buckled the latigo straps. He could feel the heat of Bella Mae's stare as he straightened, and he kind of half listened for the stamp of her foot. "Sometimes I think I *hate* you," she breathed; and he said:

"Who you tryin' to fool now?"

She heard the laughter in his voice and she cursed him, heavy breasts stirring under the sway of her passions. "Are you *crazy?*" she flared. "There ain't a one of those men will forget you — there ain't one that'll rest till he's evened the score!"

He fished a pair of Spanish spurs from his saddlebags, buckled them onto his boots and stood up again. He looked at her then, one eyebrow raised quizzically, a half wondering look breaking out of his stare. "D'you know," he said suddenly, "you're a damn' pretty baggage!"

He reached out a hand and pulled her against him, bent his head down and kissed her. Some emotion rushed through him that was close to savagery. She could feel the touch of it — was startled but responded. Then she stood quite still, staring up at him, breathless, bruised lips a little parted.

He said gruffly: "I'm sorry, Bella."

Then she struck him. More bitterly outraged than she had ever been, she struck him wildly, hotly, with a fierce and panting fury. Again and again she struck him till she had no strength left for it; then she shoved him against his horse. "Get out!" she gritted huskily — "get out an' don't come back!"

He rode two solid hours before he got that scene out of mind. There was shame in the heavy plodding of his blood, and a furious contempt for his conduct. The girl had gone out of her way to help him; she had warned him — tried to keep him out of this mess; and he had treated her like an alley cat.

He fiddled with his reins, the lines of his cheeks turned dour with his thinking; but gradually the grandeur, the impressive majesty of this broad open land lifted him out of his mood and he looked around, pleased, fully liking what he saw.

This was *his* country — *cow country;* he was glad to be back. He had been too long a time out of it. God had meant man to live in the open, not to bake out his guts under kerosene lamps.

Yesterday he had believed himself running from destiny; now he saw things with a clearer perspective. Not from himself had he tried to run, but from the curse of those honky-tonk towns that had known him — that interminable succession of gambling dives and barrooms to which the feud at Smith's Crossing had exiled him. Month after month he'd searched for cow ranch employment only, at last, to realize the truth. The word had gone out: *Have no truck with Mark Connifay!* Smith's Crossing had done that; fear of his guns had done its best to slam him onto the outlaw trail. Root hog or die.

Mark had lived. As a gambler. But now he was done with gambling. He was back to the good clean soil again; and he meant to stay, come high water or hell.

Off to the left the green of willows marked the course of a stream. Adobe buildings hugged the shade of their branches and these, he thought, would be headquarters for Kroniac's Fiddle-Back Ranch.

Connifay nodded approvingly. Good layout. Good range. Running water from the hills.

There was much about this business which he did not understand, but one thing he understood clearly. Timpas was cooking up something. The white-hatted man hadn't fooled him; he might pull the wool over some folks' eyes, but he wasn't fooling Mark Connifay. A "buggy boss," Bella Mae had called him, meaning an Eastern man who gave his orders from a wagon because his seat didn't care for the feel of a saddle; but the girl was wrong. Such might well be his pose, and he dressed the part, but the Wet Moon boss was no Easterner. Which argued he was up to something, very probably crooked, which would see blood spilled before he got done with it. Else why had he tried to hire Mark Connifay?

Mark was in no doubt the man knew him. Bannock had remembered. Bella Mae had tabbed him. Shain had obviously had his hunches; and so had Timpas — else why had he offered such unheard-of wages, capped with the promise of a bonus, to a gambling man for work on a cow ranch?

It just didn't jell. The man knew him.

Since he couldn't hire him, it was quite in the cards that Timpas might endeavor to arrange that nobody else should.

Connifay's lips streaked a tight little grin.

The sun's heat flicked sparkles from the purling stream that made faint gurgle behind the ranch's buildings. There was a long, squat house with a shady veranda on which, at the moment, two men stood talking. Farther over was the bunkhouse, or "dice house" as it was sometimes called. Yonder was the "swallow-an'-git-out trough," as the cook's domain, here a separate shanty, might quite possibly be known. Back of these were the outbuildings, a barn, two privies, harness shed and blacksmith shop. Peeled-pole corrals lay off to one side. You could always tell the main one, no matter how large or small it might be, by the snubbing post that was in its center. There was even a "crowding pen" — a smaller corral into which critters could be shunted for branding and gotching. Between these was the "squeeze," a chute frequently utilized for the branding of older cattle.

Connifay looked again toward the ranch house. The men on the veranda were watching him. He rode over and politely stayed on his horse till the older man growled, "Howdy. Fall off an' cool your saddle, stranger."

"Don't care if I do," smiled Connifay, and tossed his reins across the peeled hitching rail.

The man who had spoken looked upwards of sixty; his tall, spare figure and grizzled cheeks proclaimed the veteran cowman. His hair was white, but there was plenty of life in the glance he gave Connifay. His lip didn't curl, but you got that impression. There was little doubt of his opinion of gamblers.

"Grub'll be ready shortly," he said. "Make yourself to home. Kroniac's my name, and this is the Fiddle-Back — my spread," he mentioned in a way that left no doubt what he thought of it. "This is Buffalo Grote, my range boss."

Connifay nodded. The high, stiff frame of Buffalo Grote settled back on its bootheels.

"I've most gen'rally noticed," Grote said plainly, "when a man don't give out his name there's a reason."

"More often than not that's the case," agreed Connifay. "And when you see a gent that don't like strangers it's a pretty safe bet he's got back-trail-itis. I'm not packin' any *tin*, if that's what's fussin' you."

"You tryin' to start somethin' with me?" Grote demanded.

Connifay's eyes held a cold, bright malice. "If the boot fits, Grote, pull it on," he said.

Grote stared with his wind-burned

31

cheeks locked tightly. He came a half step forward and abruptly stopped. It was remarkable to see, the way his cheeks changed color. His eyes slewed away and he backed off the porch. The sound of his boots died across the yard.

There was a tremendous interest in old Kroniac's stare. He said, "You ever punched cattle?" and Connifay smiled.

"I've choused a few."

"Ever considered doin' it again?"

"I might . . . under certain conditions."

"I guess you wouldn't be interested."

"In what?"

"In workin' for me," old Kroniac said. "I'd like to put you on here. I liked the way you just handled Grote. He's gettin' a little mite chesty lately."

Connifay said nothing. They sat awhile in silence. "Of course," the rancher said, "I couldn't offer you much. With the market what it is, an' one thing and another. I ain't fixed good as usual right now. But I could use you here, boy — I sure could use you."

He rasped a gnarled hand across his chin, eyed Connifay slanchways. But whatever it was he was working up to say, the cook interrupted it by banging on his dishpan.

"Come'n git it," he yelled, " 'fore I slop it to the hawgs!"

Grub finished, Connifay rolled him up a cigarette and, sauntering across to the bunkhouse, joined a couple of the Fiddle-Back punchers who were squatted in its shade. Their names, it appeared, were Jawbone and Studhoss, and, as is usually the case with cowboys, their talk was of horses and women. Studhoss said his lady friend was "pretty as a basket o' chips." Jawbone grunted scornfully, " 'Pretty'!" he said. "Why, that girl's ugly as a Mexican sheep — you wouldn't know pretty if it popped you in the eye! In the first place, she's bigger'n a eight-mule wagon —"

"Whaddayou mean 'big'?" Studhoss growled.

"Well, I wouldn't wanta git pers'nal, but — Well, hell, take her face!"

"Whatsa matter with her face?"

"She's so narrer between the horns she c'ld look through a needle with both eyes to oncet!"

"Whatsa matter with that? You said she was *big*," complained Studhoss. "There ain't nothin' big about lookin' through a needle."

"Her feet're big, ain't they? She's got

more hoof'n that Texican, Wallace —"

"I druther hev her feet," sniffed Studhoss, "than —"

"How many riders drawin' pay from this outfit?"

Studhoss, turning, eyed Connifay coldly. Jawbone, squinting off across the range, said: "Don't you reckon, Studhoss, it's nigh about time Miz' Ann was gittin' back?"

Connifay took no offense; he had expected to be snubbed. A stranger asking questions in this kind of country was liable to find himself looking down a gun barrel. He had known that when he cut into their talk. But nothing ventured, nothing gained; and at the back of his mind an idea was shaping. He said:

"Reason I asked, two different parties made me an offer last night. Both parties ran cow spreads."

"Mebbe they was huntin' new blood f' their stud games."

That was Studhoss. But Jawbone, hunkered on his boot-heels, was carving meaningless ruts in the sand. "Mebbe," he said, cocking his head at the marks, "they took you f' one of Curly Bill's bunch. He's been operatin' over round Shakespeare."

Connifay said, "One of them was right

determined. Offered me a hundred an' twenty a month. Plus bonuses."

Both punchers picked up their ears, exchanging significant glances.

"Timpas!" growled Studhoss; and Jawbone unloaded some brown tobacco. "You never can tell," he said darkly, "which way a pickle will squirt when y' grab it."

"Mighty good loafin' weather," Connifay drawled, and observed the hot flush that licked up their cheekbones. "I was just wonderin' —"

"Grote put your name in the time book, Mister?"

"If he has he ain't told me."

"Then you better keep right on wonderin' —"

"*An'*," Jawbone growled, "there's a lot better places you c'ld do it in — savvy?"

Connifay grinned, but knew he was done here. There was the sound of a wagon coming down the road, but no one turned to see who was coming. Both men were eying him suspiciously, and Jawbone's regard was plainly hostile. There was also Grote to be reckoned with. Better be off while the way was open.

He got up and shook the kinks from his muscles. "Nice meetin' you, boys. Give my regards to all inquirin' friends."

Quick as a flash Jawbone said: "What do you want we should say to the sheriff?"

"Just tell him you saw me lookin' well — an' the name is Connifay, 'case he asks."

The wagon sound was much closer now. Someone was coming like hellity larrup. But Mark crossed to the house without looking around. It might be Grote; Grote had not eaten with them.

He lifted the reins and reached for the saddlehorn. The wagon was coming into the yard, by the sound. Studhoss called something that was drowned in its rumble. Lifted dust rushed across the yard; the wagon stopped with a screech of brake blocks. Connifay, shrugging, swung into his saddle.

On impulse then, he turned and looked round.

A girl was getting down from the wagon. Lithe she was, and slender, willowy. The clustered ringlets of her windblown hair gleamed like spun metal where the sun's light touched them. She lifted her head and Connifay stared.

He had left this girl at Smith's Crossing. "You cheap tinhorn," she had told him, "you ought to be *hanged* — shootin's a sight too good for you!"

4. Bannock Rides Out His String

It was she all right! Too well he remembered that proud-goddess look; the deep, hazel eyes of her, the rich, tawny hair brushed away from her forehead. And those expressive red lips —

He cut loose of his thinking. She'd remembered him. The look of her eyes had gone wide and dark — startled, and she stood there regarding him with a stiff erectness, one hand at her breast as though to still its tumult. She had a right to know tumult! to know consternation! He saw the turbulence of her, the bright, slashing anger.

She moved toward him.

He saw the punchers' heads turn curiously; and then forgot them.

She stopped by his stirrup; and all the memories of their single meeting rushed back to him, mocking, deriding him, branding as false that look of rugged honesty which had seemed so integral a part of her. There was no honesty in her.

She said: "What are you doing here?

Why have you followed me?"

"Followed you!" He laughed shortly. "I suppose you've come to warn me out of *this* country, too!"

"I asked you a question. Are you going to answer me, or do I have to call —"

"Call an' be damned! I notice you called quick enough when I quit Smith's Crossing!"

"You — you contemptible cur!" Outrage flattened her cheeks — put its flush on them; she forgot all about being a proud blonde goddess. She snatched loose the quirt that hung from his pommel. Twice its humming end curled round his head. His hat tumbled off and there was blood on his face as the blue roan, snorting, shied away from her anger.

She stood back, panting, her wild eyes still blazing, as he got off the horse and picked up his beaver. With lips locked whitely, he got into the saddle.

Voice brittle with passion, she said: "I'm Ann Kroniac. This is the Fiddle-Back Ranch — my father's. Never come back here as long as you live!"

Had a man tried what that girl had just done, he'd have stopped a blue whistler. Connifay would have yanked out a pistol and killed the man. But a woman was different.

You couldn't lay hands on a woman.

One thing, though — she needn't to worry about him coming back!

He had just about decided he would accept old Kroniac's offer; would pitch in and do what he could to save the Fiddle-Back for him, for it had become pretty obvious to Connifay that it was the Fiddle-Back Timpas was after, and only one thing he could possibly think of could explain why Kroniac hands, at a time like this, should be lazing around at the outfit's headquarters. Grote, the Kroniac range boss, was selling them out to Timpas. There was no other answer possible.

Though it was none of his funeral, he'd been going to help them. He *had* been going to. Now, wild horses couldn't drag him back. Let them lose their ranch and to hell with them!

When the lees of his anger cleared from his stare he was miles away and his horse was lathered. He had no idea of his whereabouts; the sun had set and yucca forms made lonely, sentinel shapes in the shadows. The hush of this somber land enwrapped him. The western peaks were black, and sharp as jagged glass they lay against the dimming orange sky while to the east the towering Organs, blue slate in the fading afterglow, were hardly discernible. Due south the country rolled away in a chaos of broken hills and washes. Somewhere in that desolation Single Cinch would light its lamps.

A red moon lifted, and Connifay's thoughts conjured up the face of Kroniac's daughter. He could think of her now without temper — with a kind of pity almost; and the set of his lips framed a twisted grin as he felt of the welts she'd raised with his quirt.

He wondered what could have taken her to faroff Smith's Crossing, to a place so remote in distant Texas; he tried to fit what he knew of her into that setting. He'd supposed at the time she was living there, but this, as seen now, was palpably false. She might have been visiting someone there. Or she might have been there on business — Fiddle-Back business for Old Man Kroniac. He could remember his own moves plainly.

It was one of those times when he'd been at loose ends. Not down on his luck, but fed up with gambling and all that went with it. He'd been within thirty-five miles of the town and sentiment had taken him over; a mawkish hankering that had very nearly cost him his life.

Three men he had known in the old carefree days had spotted him ere he'd been in the town ten minutes. He'd met them en masse as he was tying his horse to a hitch rack. They'd stared; sort of startled, and then, without so much as a nod or a "Howdy!" had scuttled across the street as if their last hope of heaven depended upon how swiftly they got out of his sight. Like wildfire the news had sped through Smith's Crossing: *"Mark Connifay's back! He's wearin' his gun!"* He could hear the excited whispers now, as plainly as though he were on that street.

And that had been when he had met Ann Kroniac. He hadn't known what her name was then. She was just a girl who stopped in front of him grimly, square in the center of that empty street. A proud-looking girl with hate in her eyes. And she'd lit right into him. Hadn't he spilled enough blood around there already? Did he have to start it up again three years later? Didn't he think life had *any* value? Oh, she'd poured it into him all right. Seemed it was a crime his kind were allowed to run loose; he'd judged she figured him a kind of mad dog that someone ought to chain up and shoot. Only shooting hadn't seemed to appeal to her either. "You cheap tinhorn," she'd cried hotly, "you ought to be hanged — shooting's a sight too good for you!"

He'd asked her if she'd any suggestions. It had been like throwing dead leaves on a bonfire. A regular sod-pawing mood she'd got into. He could haul his freight, and haul it right then, or she'd get her uncle out after him! Who was her uncle — Well, he'd find out if he didn't make tracks. Her uncle was a man who believed in law and order — who knew what to do with mad dogs like him. Silver Dollar Joe, he was called, and — That had been quite enough for Mark Connifay. Too plainly he recalled the clutch of those moments. Silver Dollar Joe was sheriff, it appeared; but in the old days Silver Dollar had been a hired-gun hombre on the side Mark had licked in that water-rights fracas — Silver Dollar and Fisher and Bannock and Thompson, and a lot of lesser gun fighters whose names he'd forgotten. If Silver Dollar was sheriffing that country, it was no place for a Connifay to do any lingering.

The girl had said if he'd turn his horse and leave plumb immediate, she'd undertake to keep Silver Dollar at home. So he'd left; and spent the next two weeks trying to shake Silver Dollar, who had *not* stayed home by a good long ways!

Thinking it over as he rode through the dusk, it seemed highly likely to Connifay that the girl had gone over there to enlist Joe's aid. Which augured old Kroniac was in no sense blind to what Ely Timpas was cooking up here. Which augured something else, of very direct import to one Mark Connifay — but he shrugged the thought away, recalling what Timpas had told him last night: "There'll be no neutrals cluttering up this valley. Those who aren't for me will be figured *against* me, and dealt with accordingly."

Connifay nodded. It might be so. But he was through with running.

The moon was now filled to a yellow roundness and somewhere, a coyote's howl deepened the lonely feeling of this land. It was a dream splashed with silver — a dream of something that could never be; and Mark Connifay sighed. All his bones were tired and he ached with an inexpressible longing that was somehow tied up with the face of Ann Kroniac; and all his thinking had turned wistful and hopeless.

He remembered then the long supple shape of Bella Mae Brady . . . the painted curve of her lips . . .

He was back. The lamps of Single Cinch dappled the horse-tracked dust of the road. A piano pounding and the shrill wail of a fiddler's bow poured discord through the night's felted gloom. He had slept last night at the Cap and Ball, in one of those cubbyholes off the balcony; in spite of the noise he hoped to sleep there tonight. And that way, dog-tired, with his guards all down and drained of feeling, he racked his horse before the resort and stiffly climbed from the saddle.

Yonder, before the blacksmith shop, a huddle of men turned and looked his way. Someone stood in the saloon-front's shadows. Across the way someone softly called: "Mark! Oh, Mark — wait!"

It was Bella Mae's voice; but uncaring, unthinking, too tired to wonder why a girl who only that morning had hated him so intensely should now be calling him, he mounted the steps and pushed through the batwings.

Only then did he realize how quiet the place was. No piano, no fiddle, disturbed the tense hush. Their stand was against this street-front wall and, looking along it,

Connifay saw two shrinking girls in dance-hall costume crouched beside a scared-white fiddler. With narrowing eyes he turned toward the bar.

It was black with the shapes of waiting men.

A swagger step drew his eyes to the balcony. Bannock was there. He was grinning with triumph.

A tiny settling of Connifay's cheeks was the only sign that he sensed his danger.

"What is this, Bannock — some kind of a play?"

"Yeah," Bannock said, and his tone showed enjoyment. "We're playin' *The Last of Mark Connifay*. It's goin' to be good."

"It'll have to be." Connifay's contemptuous glance raked the bar crowd. "I don't think much of your supportin' cast. You better postpone it till you get better actors."

Bannock laughed, short and reckless. "We're playin' it now."

But Connifay shook his head. "Better not. As the star of this piece I got a right to demand experienced talent."

"But you ain't the star of this piece," Bannock leered. "Fact is, we got you down for the corpse, an' —"

"Seems quite a passel of others wants to have that part. Some of these boys're lookin' right determined. If they don't cut loose of them gun handles pronto, three-four of them anyway is goin' to lose fingers."

The silence turned thin and cold as water.

"You're a cur dog, Bannock, takin' scraps from Timpas' table."

Bannock licked dry lips. He stood a moment longer, staring, his narrowed eyes boring into Connifay's. He let his breath out, shrugged, turned away — and came slamming round, with a six-gun lifted.

A mirthless grin wreathed Connifay's face. Flame tore a white streak, jabbing upward; a drift of smoke blurred the lines of his body. Gun sound hammered the walls of the place. It was the only sound heard for long, long moments.

A groan welled from Bannock. A spasm jerked his gaunt shape forward and toppled him over the balcony railing. He was dead when he hit the barroom floor.

The crowd stared rigidly, nerves stretched taut, their faces frozen.

Across that hush came Timpas' yell. "What in God's name is going on here?"

5. A Voice in the Forest

"I've been showing these gentlemen how to make corpses. You'll be interested in this. It might save you some money."

Timpas' narrowed glance passed from Connifay's tight-smiling face to the big, smoking pistol gripped so carelessly in his hand; passed back again while he slowly stiffened and an angry red came into his features. Then he followed the direction of Connifay's gesture and a startled pallor broke across his cheeks. "Good Lord!" he cried in mingled rage and fear. "Cash Bannock! Have you killed him?"

"You ought to know, Timpas. Mebbe this'll be a lesson to the rest of your gunpackers. Mebbe you'd like a demonstration yourself?"

There was shock in Timpas' tautened stance. It looked for a moment as though he were going to be sick. His face was blotched and poisonously bloated and great beads of sweat brightly glistened on his forehead. Then he must have remembered who he was in this country. His face got dark and then he grinned with his teeth. "You're aiming that chin music in the wrong direction —"

"I think not."

"You can think what you please. I have never paid Bannock one penny for anything. Here," Timpas sneered, "is the man to throw that at," and he moved from the door, letting in a man who'd been waiting back of him. "There's your range boss, Tod. Better get him out of here."

The rippling grace of a panther marked the newcomer's movements. His eyes were dark brown, liquid and luminous, seeming almost black so large were their pupils. His somber glance showed a bright intentness as it passed over Connifay; and the pale knife scar that ran from chin up to cheekbone along the left side of his unsmiling face stood out like a brand as Timpas stepped back and let him see Cash Bannock.

"There's your range boss," Timpas grinned, "and here's the tinhorn that rubbed him out for you."

The panther man's hands were hooked in his gun belt. His eyes were round, unwinking bores that were tunneling through Connifay; and the atmosphere of the room got tighter and tighter.

Connifay said, "You reckon you'll know me?"

"If we meet again? Yeah, I'll know you, friend." He gestured toward Bannock, "What was it — cards?"

Connifay punched the spent cartridge from his pistol, thrust in a fresh one and returned the weapon to the shoulder harness he wore under his coat. His eyes considered the man inscrutably. "No," he said, "it wasn't cards."

The panther man said, "My name's Tod Hackberry. I run the Currycomb. That target of yours was my range boss. I got a right to know what happened to him."

"Sure." Connifay smiled a little, insolently, "You can see, can't you?"

Hackberry said, "Take it easy — take it easy, friend. I'm not hunting trouble. All I want is the truth."

Connifay said, not changing the tone of his voice by the slightest, "They was stagin' a play. Bannock, and that bunch of plug-uglies you see by the bar. It was to be called *The Finish of Mark Connifay* or some such smartness. Bannock allowed there was goin' to be a rub-out." He paused to smile into Hackberry's eyes. "I made sure he wasn't disappointed."

There was a moment of silence; then —

"He's a damn' liar!" snarled a cadaverous man among the crowd by the bar. "We was waitin' around f' the games to get started. Cash stepped out on that balcony up there, an' 'fore he knew what was happenin' this tinhorn grabbed iron an' blasted him!"

Connifay's grin showed his hard white teeth. He lifted his beaver. "Admiration of your gall," he said, and looked around at Hackberry. "You can take whichever story you like."

"Well," Timpas said, drawing on his gloves, "he's your range boss, Hackberry. I'll have to get along. Good night, gentlemen."

Hackberry waited till the swing doors quit squeaking. Then he said very soft, his dark eyes hard on Connifay: "I'm goin' to give you a tip, friend. Get out of this country before somebody plants you."

Connifay shrugged, turned, and mounted the stairs.

The swamper fixed Connifay's breakfast next morning, and while he ate, the man watched him brightly. "I took care of your horse las' night," he said. "I left him down at the stable — Jed Hankins' livery."

"Much obliged."

"That's all right. Glad to do it. I knowed

you'd forgot 'im. Man couldn't hardly blame you; though if I'd been the one that had done that shootin', I'd of sure crawled my horse an' lit out pronto."

"Mister Hackberry told me it might be a good idea."

"He wa'n't kiddin' you, neither," declared the swamper, and picked up his mop with a shake of the head. "He won't be forgettin' you, mister."

After he'd finished eating, Connifay shoved back his chair and lighted his third cigar of the day; he'd smoked two already to curry up an appetite.

It was a fine large morning with a cool breeze drifting off the desert. Connifay, leaving the saloon, strolled about for a look at the town. There wasn't much to it. Like most of its kind it was crude and garish. The stage company's buildings, a general store with forty-'leven prices, the saloon, a hoofshaper's shop and eight or ten pine-log shanties. And Jed Hankins' Livery Stable & Corral. The sun was getting hot when he stopped by the corral to look over Hankins' horses.

He had his own horse saddled and was leading the blue from the stable when the proprietor put in an appearance. Connifay tossed him a dollar.

"Pullin' out, eh?" smiled Hankins. "Well, I'm bound to say you stuck it out longer'n I figured you would. She's a hard, hard country, stranger."

Connifay shrugged, and took the west trail out.

The distant Sierra Caballos showed dark and clear in the morning light. The range stretched before him, brightly patterned with sunlight and shadow. A number of men looked after him curiously as he rode out of town, then convened at the stable to compare notes with Hankins. "A tinhorn mebbe," said the blacksmith to Hankins, "but a damn tough buck from all accounts. An' fast! — did you see that draw of his last night? Slickest thing I ever clapped eyes on!" Hankins said: "That fella's no gambler;" and the stage company's man said, "He sure ain't!" emphatically. "He's made enemies of 'most every man he's bumped into. That ain't gamblin' — it's suicide. I'd sure like to know what his game is."

The hoof-shaper smiled at them pityingly. "I'll tell you lunkheads. That fella's a Canadian River man come out here to look into this rustlin'."

It was in Connifay's mind to ride the valley's west side today. Yesterday he'd quartered its eastern edge. Tomorrow — well, a man never knew about tomorrow; but if he was going to stay in this country it behooved him to know its landmarks, the location of its ranches. This in simple self-defense, for this country's breed didn't like him and there might come a time when knowing this range would spell the difference between six feet of earth and continued living. The denizens of this country were a tough and hard-hating breed by the look of things, and he kind of thought he'd stick around if only to show how light he held their advice and opinions. They were a sight too anxious to see him gone to suit Mark Connifay's state of mind.

Rim to rim the hemming mountains bounded the valley north, east and west — an empire of grass, of rolling prairies, of alkali flats, of lava beds, of sugarloaf hills green-spangled with forests; and off to the south, mile on shimmering mile of heat, ran the desert, glaring white, to the cobalt blue of the Mexican mountains.

Yes, Connifay thought, this was the land for him. Mere bigness had never impressed him; he had been in places far larger than this sweeping valley, yet he drew a deep breath and his eyes showed a pride and eagerness as they considered its tawny distances. The smell of this land was in his nostrils. Like a captive bronc suddenly freed of its hobbles, he was savoring its rank flavor; and the pungency of it tugged at him, striking a responsive chord somewhere deep in his nature. The call of this land was summoning him, and he flung up his head, sniffing hungrily, lips peeled back in a thin queer smile, while an excitement and an eagerness he had not known in years rushed tumultuously through him.

This was his land.

He had no illusions about its breed. They were, for the most part, outlaws; long riders, riffraff, renegades and worse. There was no possible chance of peace — of continued peace — between them, no trust or reasonableness or mercy. Pride and trickery and black deceit — these were the things God had given them as their share; these, and one thing else: grim courage. They all had courage for a hole card. The guts to play out their strings.

Deep into the tumbled hills Mark rode, and where two trails met and crossed he paused to scan a pine-slab nailed up there. Behind an arrow three sets of letters, burned with a cinch ring, pointed south. They read:

LAZY S
BRADY'S
BUG WAGON

Connifay turned his horse that way.

Within the hour he reached a wood-cutter's camp and, redirected, struck south by east over a rotting corduroy road which the big roan took with watchful care. The low drone of myriad insects made a cheerful note in the dappled shadows, and for a while he hummed a snatch of song remembered from the Crossing's cow camps. The sudden flight of some cowbirds stopped the song, left him moodily thoughtful. It was then he remembered Bella Mae Brady and the risk she had taken trying to warn him last night. It *had* been a risk; Bannock's friends wouldn't like it. Nor would Timpas or Hackberry should they happen to learn of it.

Why had she done it — called his name out that way? What had moved her to do such a rash thing when only that morning —

He stopped his horse dead, half wheeled him around and then whirled him back sharply to stare narrowly toward the fringe of the clearing where his thinking had trapped him. There was somebody coming — some rider whose shape vaguely showed through the branches. Quick fingers closed on the butt of his pistol. The rider broke from the trees.

It was Bella Mae Brady. She pulled up her horse and they stared at each other. His long, cool look pulled color into her cheeks, and with an impatient swing of her shoulders she urged her horse in closer, bringing up beside him, her left stirrup brushing his own left stirrup. She wore a bright silk blouse tucked into blue jeans whose bottoms were folded into silver-spurred range boots.

"Why didn't you stop when I called last night?"

"I've been trying to decide why you called," he told her; and she looked at him straightly.

"Is it such a problem?"

He had his answer in the gleam of her eyes, in the faint little smile that was curving her lips. In a thousand small things he could read it — but wouldn't.

She said: "You don't like me, do you?"

"Why —"

"You know what I mean."

The tone of her voice pulled his glance up sharply. Yes . . . he knew. He had seen that look on other girls' faces. He'd been afraid yesterday morning it would come to this; which was why, last night, he had not answered her.

She was watching him closely, but he did not notice.

He was trying to think how best he might tell her when, suddenly, she gave a strangled cry. Her eyes rolled wildly and she swayed in the saddle. There was time for just one thing — quick action. He leaned across her saddle, caught her; was stretched that way, every muscle straining, when a furious shout slammed across the clearing.

"By Gawd, Bella Mae! What's that tinhorn whelp tryin' t' do t' yuh?"

6. "You Don't Have to Fight Him Square —"

"You don't need that shotgun," protested the Reverend 'Lijah Bates. "When two young folks wants to git hitched up I'm accustomed to obligin' without no show of force, suh. Leave that scatter gun outside."

Old Joe Brady's bloodshot eyes considered the Reverend unpleasantly. "When I want advice outen yuh I'll ast for it." He shifted the bulge in his cheek and spat. "Meantime —"

Connifay said: "Don't you think this farce has gone far enough?"

"Farce, eh? That may be what they're callin' it now, but in my day —"

The Reverend 'Lijah cleared his throat. "Are you real sure you young 'uns —"

"What're you tryin' t' do — talk 'em outen it? 'F you think I fetched 'em — Hell's fire! Git in there an' quit argufyin' around with me 'fore I lose m' temper!"

Tall and gaunt, Joe Brady was a raw-boned, whisky-drinking product of the feuding Kentucky hills. He stilled cheap corn into liquid lightning and did considerable traffic, it was hinted, with Mescalero Apaches, what time he wasn't running guns or horses across the River below C. Jaurez. A completely unsavory customer whose red-rimmed glance had cowed persons much hardier than the frail Reverend 'Lijah.

Beneath the cued-back brim of his horsethief hat Brady's mean little eyes glowed wickedly. "Yuh goin' t' perfo'm 'er ain't yuh?" he snarled, and the Reverend Mr. Bates gave over his qualms and backed inside the house hurriedly.

"Listen, Brady," Connifay said, "I don't aim to take much more off you. You can persist in misreadin' this hand if you want to, but you won't —"

"Yuh hush an' git on in there b'fore I —"

"I've told you the truth and I'll tell you once more. Bella got sick or something and was about to fall out of her saddle. Naturally, I reached across and caught her. If you can see anything compromis— Why don't you ask *her* about —"

"I don't hev t' ast *no* one!" cursed Brady. "I know what folks's been sayin' about 'er, an' I ain't a-goin' t' hev it! I ketched yuh with 'er an' by grab yuh'll marry 'er! G'on!

Git the hell in there 'fore I bash yer golrammed face in!"

"Well?" Timpas' glare was ominous. "What've you got to say for yourself? If you can't get some action out of this crowd, I'll damn quick get me somebody who can!"

This was Timpas' town office in one of the stage company's buildings, and the cadaverous man slouched with a hip on Timpas' desk was his range boss, called simply "Fargo." If he had ever possessed an additional name none had ever heard of it. He wore crossed belts, and the pistols that sagged their tied-down holsters were sheathed butt-forward for the cross-arm draw for which he was locally famous.

He grinned at Timpas sourly. "That gunslick tinhorn, mebbe," he said, and guffawed when Timpas came angrily half out of his chair. "Sit down — sit down," Fargo told him. "I've got that fella all fixed up for you —"

"Fixed up?"

"You bet. I've got him took care of *right*."

Timpas' eyes held a steely glitter. "What do you mean 'took care of'?"

"Just what I said. How much'd you promise Bannock?"

"I never promised him nothin'!"

"You better watch your language, Ely, or some of these boys'll be wonderin' about you. A Easterner would shoot hisself before he'd mix talk the way you do. Howsomever — about this tinhorn. You know how Ol' Man Kroniac is — what he thinks about cards an' loose women, I mean. Well, I got things fixed now so he wouldn't hire that fella if he was the las' guy this side of Jericho."

"Well," Timpas snarled, "what is it — a secret?"

"No," Fargo guffawed, "it's too good to keep. I fixed up a deal with Ol' Brady; he's goin' to splice Bella Mae to the tinhorn —"

"You fool!" Timpas jumped to his feet, eyes blazing. "What the hell kind of play —"

"Take it easy," Fargo drawled. "You been chewin' your toenails f' fear this tinhorn would hook up with Kroniac. You reckon Kroniac would ever hire a gamblin' man what had tied hisself up with a —"

Timpas held up a hand in quick warning. There was somebody coming through the warehouse. Fargo wheeled off the desk with his left hand dropping; but it was only the stable boy who worked for Hankins. "She's here — at the general store," he said; and Timpas' look was a cold, dark thing.

When the boy had gone, Fargo said: "Ann Kroniac. I tooled her in for the tinhorn's weddin'. She don't like Connifay anyhow, an' when she hears what he's into now . . ." He spread his hands with a knowing grin; but Timpas caught up something out of his talk.

"How do you know she don't like him?"

"He was out to the Fiddle-Back yestiday. Grote says she took a quirt to him." Fargo spat in the direction of a cuspidor. "If a woman —"

Timpas scowled him silent. "Lemme think a minute." The gleam of his teeth came through his lips. Then abruptly, his scowl deepening, he swore. "I mighta known there was a catch in this some place! You're leavin' Bella Mae out of your —"

Fargo said: "I don't leave *any*body outa my figgerin'. *She* won't kick. I was in the stable when he got his horse yestiday. She came round while he was cinchin' up. They passed a few words an' he grabbed her an' kissed 'er. Then he 'pologized. I'm here t' say she slapped him proper."

"And you think," Timpas stared, "she'll —"

62

"Like a shot!" Fargo chuckled, and put some more juice in the cuspidor. He looked up at Timpas slanchways. "You got a lot to learn about women, Ely." He ignored Timpas' scowl with bland amusement. "By the way, young Tony's at the Cap'n Ball — buckin' the tiger ag'in, like usual. How much longer you figgerin' t' stake him?"

Timpas, big, willful, intolerant of any views but his own, said irritably: "Suppose you let *me* take care of that. Meantime, what about those options you were s'posed to pick up? Have you got 'em? — Why ain't you? What do you think we're payin' you for? Six months, by grab! an' all you've got us is two lousy quit-claims to one-horse outfits we was bound to get anyhow! You were s'posed to be *tough!* Tough!" Timpas snorted. "What've you done about Shain?"

Fargo got up and took his thumbs from the armholes of his vest. "Any time I don't suit your book you can get somebody else to do your skull draggin'." He looked at the big man sourly. "It appears to me that two-by-four tinhorn has done got into your hair, Mister Timpas."

Timpas pulled up his chin. He said very softly: "You was in that crowd when he tunneled Bannock. Mebbe your wolf was sick last night?"

"Mebbe it was feelin' about like yours when you passed the deal to Currycomb. Fella'd thought you had a real pressin' engagement —"

Timpas came out of his chair with a snarl. His grip lashed out and spun the gun fighter round. Fargo's back shook the wall as he reeled against it, and Timpas was bringing a big fist up when Fargo, white and shaken and pinned there as he was, gritted huskily: "Get your damn' hands off me — *get 'em off!*" And Timpas, his wild glare raking downward, saw the bright wing of metal jutting out from Fargo's waist.

He backed away, teeth glinting.

"I ain't your dog," whispered Fargo smokily. "I work for you because it suits my book; but I ain't no hound to be kicked around an' you'd better remember it. You had better remember it," he repeated thinly.

Timpas, silent, made a vast and burly shape against the light coming in at the window back of him. He regarded Fargo with a long, still look; then his shoulders lifted in brusque impatience. "Forget it," he said, and wheeled back to the table.

Fargo watched him go.

He poured a stiff drink from the bottle standing on it; poured another, looked up and pushed the bottle toward Fargo.

But the range boss stood with his gun still in hand. His cold little eyes were bright and suspicious.

Timpas gave him a nervous catlike glance. "Get hold of Grote for me — tell him I want him. On your way out of town, drop by the saloon and send Tony over here — Shain, too, if you see him. And send Jackson in if he's back at the ranch. That's all. Shut the door."

After Fargo had gone, the Wet Moon boss thrust big hands deep in the pockets of his coat and took a few savage turns of the room. He'd been a fool last night to show his face at the Cap and Ball — a double-damned fool; first to put any trust in Bannock and second to go over there to look at Connifay's corpse! And he'd been a bigger fool, just now, to let his temper crowd him into jumping Fargo. The man was a snake — and just as deadly. But he'd been right about one thing — too damnably right. Connifay *was* in his hair! Wherever he looked the gambler's chilled-steel eyes were there looking back at him.

The man was become an obsession! An incubus!

Timpas had lied when he'd told Fargo the past six months had gained them nothing but quit-claims on a couple of small outfits. The past six months had gained Timpas plenty, but he did not propose to make others aware of this till he had this valley in the palm of his hand. He had strengthened his grip in a hundred ways; had consolidated his position until there was now but a matter of days between himself and the coveted prize he'd been working for.

But a kind of grim dread had seized him, dread directly traceable to the advent of Connifay. Who was he? *What* was he? Why had he come here? The damnable uncertainty hung over the Wet Moon boss like a curse. There was a sufficient uncertainty inherent in his venture without having the threat of this gambler added to it.

"Gambler!"

Timpas gritted the word as though he would have liked to choke it. The man probably *was* a gambler; but not in the sense he would have folks believe. He was something more than a cardsharper, and it was this that had got its claws into Timpas. The suspicious eyes of the Wet Moon boss had observed how tight was the fit of that coat, how it cramped the swing of the man's broad shoulders. Nor had he missed the scars on the man's powerful hands. And there were other things. The bronzed, wind-whipped cheeks of him, the stubborn jaw; the whole brash look of his high, flat face. The kind of face you'd expect in a cow country — but not hunched back of a faro bank!

Timpas' scowl held a sultry fury. The man had to be dealt with, and promptly, before his meddling uncovered something vital, something dangerously inimical to Timpas' plans. Already the gambler's brittle smile had lost Timpas face. Whatever was to be done would have to be swift and decisive; it must neither fail nor connect Ely Timpas with the man's undoing.

Fargo's way crossed his mind, and Timpas' lips curled derisively. The plans of a fool! You could put no trust in them; you *dared* not — there were too many factors against success. Whatever the way, it had to result in the man's death. *Death* — that was it!

A crunch of boots beyond the front door jerked Timpas round with his eyes slit-narrow.

It was only Hackberry. The Currycomb

boss smiled thinly. "Matter, Ely? Conscience botherin' you?"

Timpas raked him with an intolerant glance, took the hand from his coat and crossed to the desk. He poured a stiff drink, wiped his lips, corked the bottle. "Well? What is it?" he growled. "I'm a busy man, Hackberry."

"You looked busy last night. What were you tryin' to do? Get me tangled with that fella?"

Timpas pulled up his chin. "Are you tryin' to be funny?"

"On the contrary. I was never more in earnest. I want to know what your idea was. Tryin' to get me fitted for a coffin mebbe?"

Timpas assayed a laugh that fell flat. This Currycomb boss was bad medicine, and Timpas was not at his best this evening. He decided to tell the truth. "I couldn't very well admit an interest in Bannock —"

"Bannock's been takin' your money for quite a spell, Ely."

Timpas didn't like the tone of those words. It turned his cheeks a little flushed and angry. He said: "I made you a damn good offer —"

"An' I turned it down."

Timpas brushed that aside. "I've a better one for you —"

"Mebbe I ain't interested. It might just be that I *like* this country."

"Now you *are* bein' funny," Timpas said. "Hell, let's talk turkey; I'll put my cards on the table. This Wet Moon syndicate's a growing concern. I needn't bore you with a lot of fool details; the crux of the matter is that we need more range — we need a *lot* more range. The Eastern owners have been doin' some speculating; they've bought up a hell's smear of cattle an' they expect me to feed them. I've wired 'em just what the situation is here an' they've give me permission to make you what I'm bound to say is a damn good offer."

"Yeah?" Hackberry's look showed his opinion of syndicates. "Playin' Santa Claus, eh? How much've you worked 'em up to? Ten cents on the dollar?"

"We'll pay you twenty thousand dollars for your holdings and you can stay on as manager at a hundred an' fifty. I guess," Timpas grinned, "that ought to show who your friend is."

Hackberry stared. Plainly the syndicate boss had surprised him. He said, "It sounds all right. . . ."

"Sounds!" Timpas scowled. "It *is* all

right! Nobody else will ever pay you that much; an' I'm bound to say we won't, very long. You've got a week to make up your mind in. After that the whole deal is off. There are plenty of others will be glad to deal with us."

Hackberry smiled, and the smile angered Timpas. He said, coldly wicked: "It's quite in the cards we'll get your spread anyway. There are a lot of resources back of this syndicate, and some of the owners," he added darkly, "would a heap rather *take* range than pay for it. Just a word to the wise, Tod."

Not long after Hackberry left, the scrape of a boot rasped through the evening quiet and Timpas, knowing that sound, hitched up his trousers, put his feet on the desk and was smoking a cigar when the newcomer entered. He was a weak-faced young fellow with a dragging foot and untrustworthy eyes that looked worried and sullen. He was Kroniac's son, ill-tempered, unduly.

Timpas said, "Hello, Pistol-Foot," and got a vindictive pleasure from the resentful flush that put angry spots in the girl-smooth cheeks. "You look kind of off your feed this evenin'. Have you got me that money yet?"

Tony Kroniac glared. "You know I ain't! You know how much chance I got of layin' hands —"

"You want me to go to your old man for it?"

All the color went out of the boy's pasty cheeks. His eyes searched big Timpas with a nervous dread. "Aw — damn it, Ely. I —"

"That's the trouble with you kids," Timpas told him coldly. "Always tryin' to act chesty an' nothing to back it with. Unless a man's got money, an' willin' to lose it, he's got no business getting into a poker game. What's your old man trying to do — make a gambler out of you?"

Tony felt the cruel spur of that jest too keenly to do more than stare miserably at the ranchman. His father's views touching gamblers and gambling were well known.

"Feelin' sorry for you, account of your foot an' all, a lot of damn fools," Timpas said, "have accepted your paper. They've let you get chesty, act the part of a man, when by rights you're nothing but a squirt of a kid. Which," Timpas added, "would be all right if you had any pride about you —"

"I've —"

"Don't interrupt me. You're a snivelin' kid — a whiny, snivelin', cry-baby kid; an'

71

you've got me in a jam with this gamblin'. These Santa-Claus friends of yours sometimes gamble with me. They've been doin' it lately an' payin' me off with your lousy damn paper, which I've had to take or tell 'em you're a four-flusher. Being a damn fool myself, I've taken it. But I'm in a tight spot now. As I told you last week, I've got to have that money —"

"I told you I'd get it!"

Timpas' lip curled. "But when?"

"I'll try —"

"Tryin' ain't good enough. I need it now."

"You think I can rake four hundred an' fifty dollars out of the bushes?"

"I'm not thinking; I'm *telling* you. Get me that money before tomorrow noon or I'm going out an' have a talk with your father."

"How can I?" wailed Tony. "I ain't got no friends I could borrow four hundred an' fifty dollars from!"

"Few people have," cut in Timpas dryly. "Ever try workin'?"

"Working!"

"That's the way most gents get their spare change, ain't it?"

Tony scowled. "I'd play hell gettin' four hundred an' fifty for a half a day's work —"

"Oh, I don't know," Timpas said. "There are ways. I've heard of fellows making twice that amount in a quarter of the time."

"Are you by any chance suggestin' that I stick up a bank?"

"You could always do that." Timpas grinned at him coldly. "That bank at Mesilla ought to be pretty easy. What I was thinking of, though, was the brags you been makin' about your draw-an'-shoot genius. There's plenty jobs you could get if you're good with a gun."

Tony, plainly puzzled but hopeful, said: "If you know of any, tell me."

But Timpas apparently had changed his mind. "No," he frowned, "you'd only get yourself killed. Like the rest of this town, I keep forgettin' you're a kid. Why don't you cut out a few of the Fiddle-Back steers? Your ol' man will never miss 'em."

"You mean *steal* them?" Tony gasped.

"Steal? Who said anything about stealin'? Ranch'll be yours when your ol' man dies, won't it? Then the cattle will, too. What's wrong with borrowin' a few in advance to pay your debts with? No worse'n putting bad paper in a poker game, is it?"

Tony swallowed uneasily, licked dry lips.

"But — but that would be rustlin' — rustlin' from the Fiddle-Back. I . . . I wouldn't be able to look my ol' man in the face —"

"You goin' to look him in the face when he asks you about them I.O.U.'s?"

There was a film of sweat on the boy's pale cheeks. "Ely —" his voice was hardly above a whisper. "Ely — what did you mean about — about my style with a gun?"

"The syndicate," Timpas said, "will pay four hundred an' fifty dollars — and no questions asked — to the fella that drops that tinhorn Connifay."

The boy's gleaming face looked the color of tow sack.

"What are you shakin' about?" Timpas said. "If you can use a gun there ain't nothin' to it. You don't have to fight him fair — you can drop him from the brush if you can't do it no other way."

7. Kroniac Moves

It was morning; the morning following Bannock's ill-starred attempt to plant Mark Connifay in the barroom of the Cap and Ball. On the porch of the Fiddle-Back ranch house Old Man Kroniac stared without pleasure at a neighbor he had not spoken to in fifteen years. He said: "Ride over that trail again and use a double-rigged saddle, will you?"

The hatchet face of Batista Wilkes grew surly with irritation. "Hell's fire! You better git your ears cleaned out! I said Whoa Jackson's sold to the syndicate!"

"And how did you figure that would interest me?"

"Goddlemighty!" Wilkes snarled back at him. "Ain't his holdin's above your place? Then you better watch your creek, by grab; if Timpas don't cut your water off —"

"Timpas," Old Man Kroniac said, "is a friend of mine. You're up to something, B'tiste; what is it?"

"Up t' somethin'!" Wilkes squirmed round in the saddle and turned his bitter

75

eyes on Grote. "*You* oughta know what's goin' on! What do *you* think about this Buggy-Boss Timpas?"

But Grote just stared at him woodenly and kept his buck teeth tightly shut.

Anger showed in the wrinkles of Wilkes' sallow cheeks and temper edged his wheeling stare. "So," he said to Kroniac, "Timpas is your good friend, is he? I guess Whoa Jackson is a good friend, too! You taken any count of your cattle lately?"

The tall, spare figure of the Fiddle-Back boss appeared to hunch a little forward. "I have known Ely Timpas ever since he came here, and I have always found him an upright gentleman." He judged his visitor with a cold, black glance. "I have always regretted," he added grimly, "that I cannot say as much for you."

Wilkes grinned with his teeth. "I don't pretend t' be no gentleman; but I got eyes in my head! I'm goin' to tell you somethin', Andre. It'll be somethin' f' you to think about after Wet Moon's moved you outa here. Your so-good friend, Ely Timpas, is after this whole damn valley — an' he'll get it, too, if we don't stick together. He's already bought Whoa Jackson out; an' Trindle, up in them hills back of me. An' there's five-six other spreads ready

76

to fold. If you can't see no handwritin' —"

"What has moved you to come here and tell me this?"

"What has — *Hell's fire!* What do you s'pose is goin' t' happen t' *me* after you an' this Fiddle-Back's gone?"

"Why leave out Shain and Hackberry?"

"I ain't leavin' 'em out. Shain's about ready to sell out now. But your friend has been at him — you can bet on that. As fer *you* —"

"You had some reason for coming here. You had better say what it is and get out."

The glare in Wilkes' eyes seemed to be something expected and waited for. Kroniac grew stormy. His spare frame thickened and lifted. He pointed a bony hand down the road, and his stare held the weight of a physical blow. "There's the trail, you Judas; get on it and go."

A sly and malicious hatred gleamed in the stare of Wilkes' little eyes as they probed the old man for one moment longer. He laughed shortly then and picked up his reins. "You'll be sorry fer this. You'll be sorry fer this to your dyin' day!"

Kroniac said, when Wilkes' dust had laid: "Grote, have the boys start a tally on our beef — right away."

"Sure," Grote said, "only do you think that's wise — right now, I mean? Like I told you last week, Shain an' that Wilkes are up to somethin'; they've had a guy in the rimrocks f' the past ten days. He's been watchin' this place with a glass —"

"I'll take care of him. You do what I tell you."

"Sure." Grote rasped his chin and looked at Kroniac queerly. "Only . . . well, suppose them outfits is figgerin' to jump us? What about Miz' Ann —"

"Ann's old enough to take care of herself. When Studhoss gets back from town you send him an' Jawbone out to the beef — an' keep 'em there. Understand me, Grote? For a man that's onto his business, you've a queer way of running a ranch."

Grote said nothing, but a deeper color showed behind his tan. Then his glance swung round. "Here comes Studhoss now — I'll send him right out."

"Send Jawbone, too — and the cook. Ann'll take care of my eatin' worries. An', Grote! While you're at it mebbe you better go out there yourself. Your string must be tired of the sight of this yard." He turned toward the house and left Grote staring.

Sweeping past the range boss without a

glance, Studhoss pulled up his bronc alongside the owner. "That saddle-blanket gambler that was out here yestiday killed Bannock las' night at the Cap an' Ball. One shot — plumb center!"

Kroniac wheeled in his tracks. "Keep your eye on Buff'lo." He struck off for the corral, and got his rope from the saddle. His whistling loop snared a chestnut gelding, and in almost no time he had him saddled. He took one long look around the yard, stepped into the hull and was off to the hills.

There was a glint in his eye that was strangely like anger.

8. When A Man Has To Fight

Whoa Jackson came into Single Cinch through the last red rays of a setting sun; a burly man with a windburnt face and opaque eyes that were the shade of gun steel. The horse he tied at the stage company's hitch rail was covered with dust and flecked with lather. Yet no sign of hurry marked Jackson's walk as he bowlegged his way round the sprawling warehouse and mounted the steps to Timpas' door.

He did not knock.

He opened the door with the toe of his boot, and as it banged the wall he entered sideways. He might be gullible; he was not a fool.

"Ever try knockin'?" Timpas' eyes slashed up at him roughly.

Jackson said nothing. His lips were creased in a tight, thin line. Timpas did not like the way he stood there. He said, "Here — have a chair," and shoved one across to him. Jackson stood where he was; made no move to take it.

Timpas said, "Did you get that Fiddle-Back beef across?"

Jackson smiled thinly.

"Well?" Timpas growled.

"Didn't you think I would, Ely?"

Timpas turned very still. He had no need to go beyond the man's voice, to go beyond his words or Jackson's stiff-placed shape. A danger crouched in that room, cold and deadly; a thing to be met, to be fooled or reckoned with.

"Of course," said Timpas coolly. "Only, days like these, a man never knows. Border's getting chancy —"

"Glad to hear you realize it. I got to have more dinero for this last trip, Ely. About five thousand, I guess, ought to square it."

"Square what?"

"That ambush I run into. You'll be glad to know I got your stuff across — all that Fiddle-Back stuff I stole for you; but it was sticky goin', Ely. Almost didn't cut it. Had to leave three of your outfit —"

"Thought I told you to use your own —"

"I *did* use my own boys." Jackson smiled.

"Then —"

"It was three of *your* men we left for the buzzards."

The last doubt was resolved. The watching eyes were like agate. With his cheeks stretched taut, Timpas leaned a little forward. "I don't like that —"

Jackson said: "I didn't like that ambush, either — nor the way you burned me out this noon!" There was a touch of craziness in his eyes, in the gleam of his teeth, in his slavering fury. "Go open that safe —"

"You blackmailing tramp!" Flame bit from the jerk of Timpas' hand. Dust jumped out of Whoa Jackson's vest. The slamming reports seemed to buffet him, pound him. He took one swaying, stumbling step and lost the support of his legs completely.

Timpas was calmly smoking when the crowd arrived. Jackson was dead, sprawled out on the floor, with an unfired pistol beside his fingers. Timpas told the jostling townsmen: "He was trying to sell me some Fiddle-Back beef. Damned if I can figure why he came to me, but I mighty quick told him I wasn't interested. He got scared then, I guess — tried to drag a gun on me."

Timpas' eyes held a challenge as he knocked the ash off his black cigar.

The townsmen looked at the shape on the floor; two or three shook their heads. "He ain't got no kick," the blacksmith said;

and Hankins, the liveryman, observed: "Served him right. Pretty plain now where a lot of our beef's gone. We oughta vote you a medal."

That appeared to be the consensus of opinion. Kroniac's range boss was in the crowd, and as the men filed out, Timpas said: "Couple of you boys lug him out of here, will you? Ah — you, over there; aren't you the Fiddle-Back range boss? Like to see you a minute."

When the rest had gone, Grote said: "Fargo was tellin' me —"

"Yeah." Timpas nodded. "Anything new out your way?"

"Wilkes was out this mornin'. Told the Ol' Man you was after his hide."

"What'd Kroniac say?"

"I can't figure that ol' coot noway. He didn't say nothin'. 'Tween you an' me, I think he's suspicious — I think he's been suspicious for quite a spell. He told Wilkes you was his friend; but after Wilkes left he told me to put the boys on the range. He wants a beef count."

Timpas' glance turned thoughtful. "Wants a beef count, eh?" He drummed the desk edge with spatulate fingers. "Hear anything of a fire over at Jackson's?"

Grote shook his head, but the swing of

83

his stare showed a risen interest. "Jackson say he had a fire?"

"Had an idea we burned him out."

"Mighta been Kroniac," Grote said. "He was headed toward Jackson's when he left the ranch. Wilkes claimed Jackson had sold out to you — claimed Trindle had, too. Said you'd prob'ly be dammin' the creek." Grote's bold eyes regarded Timpas curiously. "Was that right, what Wilkes said about Jackson sellin' to you?"

Quick impatience crossed Timpas' cheeks and Timpas' glance turned narrowly on Grote. A willful heat sparkled across that look, and Buffalo Grote felt his blood run cold.

"Questions," Timpas said. "That was Jackson's trouble. Always askin' questions. A wise man would find it smart to play dumb. Think it over, Grote. Roll it up with your smokin'."

Ann Kroniac, laughing across her shoulder, came out of the general store with her bundles. She moved to the edge of the railless plank porch and stopped, her body going suddenly taut. Trouble feel was plain on this street; it was an added blackness crept into its shadows. There were men on the walks, but they were not

84

moving; they were stopped, stiffly watching a group farther down.

The moments crawled by, and a feeling of something expected put a new and dangerous coolness into the breeze dropping off the Organs. A rider's spurs, scraping the porch planks, went still in midstride. A tall young fellow, just come from the saloon, chanced to glance down-street and stayed that way, rooted. A horse's fretful stamping sounded loud in the sudden stillness.

These things Ann noted subconsciously and, though hardly aware of it, knew it was Tony, her brother, who had just come out of the saloon. It was that tall and central figure of the group all eyes were watching who had caught and held her attention; that black-garbed man in the tall beaver hat.

It was the rogue who called himself Connifay — the dark-cheeked gambler from Smith's Crossing. He stood very still, coldly eying Joe Brady, who was shouting something blasphemous and wildly shaking a shotgun. And the girl standing by them, must, Ann supposed, be that Bella Mae Brady that everyone talked of; that red-headed hussy, without shame, without morals —

Ann suddenly felt her cheeks go hot. This was the story of Tony again, only now it was Connifay and Connifay was caught! Ann knew a pleased satisfaction, a malicious sense of justice well served, as she stood there watching Connifay, confusedly recalling some of the things she had heard of this girl and her wild, reckless escapades. Perversely, then, she felt almost sorry for him till she saw the quick, bright flash of his teeth — the derisively elegant gesture with which he swept off his tall beaver hat — and realized that deliberately with brazen effrontery and mockery, he was calling the whole street's attention to her.

She was coldly and instantly furious, and would have swept away — gone inside the store — but for the sudden bull bellow of Brady, who, seeing Connifay's attention diverted, had discarded his shotgun and gone leaping in, catching Connifay savagely with both hands round his throat. Connifay was bowled from his feet, and the red dust rose about their thrashing bodies. After that Ann could only stand, frozen and staring, wide-eyed and frightened, with the breath clogged tight in her throat.

She had expected this thing to be instantly over; was amazed that the dust continued to boil. How *could* the man offer resistance? How could *anyone* fight with Brady's gnarled hands wrapped so tightly round his windpipe?

Yet it was plain by the dust that the gambler *was* fighting; and the battle wasn't going all Brady's way, either. She could hear the hard panting, the grunts coming out of him, the growls and the curses. She heard one agonized whistle of breath — saw Brady lurch up and go wabbly-legged round in a floundering circle with his chest on his knees and his mouth wide open. She saw Connifay then. She hardly recognized him, so ripped were his clothes, so tattered and dust-begrimed, so twisted with rage were his dark, battered features.

Brady pulled his face up off his knee-caps. He screamed wild curses as Connifay came for him. Brady whipped out a knife that was hidden in his boot top. Connifay kicked it out of his fist.

Brady was scared now. His eyes rolled desperately as he backed away from Connifay's fists. There was blood on his face, and blood was a rattle in the wheeze of his breathing.

He seemed to know he had to grab Connifay; and, head down, he rushed again, snarling. Connifay, trying to duck, got hung up in his spurs — tripped and went over. Boots first, Brady jumped and came down with a roar. Then all was lost in the dust again, and out there someone was shouting: *"Bust 'im, Joe! Bust his guts out!"* over and over and over again. And then two shapes rolled out of the dust, locked and grunting and wildly plunging. And abruptly one came to his knees and rose with the other shape writhing in his lifted arms.

Ann jammed the back of a hand to her mouth.

The man in the air was the gambler, Connifay. Brady's purpose at once became clear. He was making for a hitch pole to break the man's back.

Dust hung thick in the darkening street; and somewhere a woman yelled: "No, Dad — *No!*" but Brady with a ghastly grin on his face continued his staggering advance on the hitch rack, and not one of that watching crowd made any attempt to check or stop him.

With all her soul Ann wished she might run, might knife this savagery out of her mind. But she could not move; she had not the strength to. The blood in her veins seemed turned to water — she could not even close her eyes, but had to stand there and stare in the clutch of horror till —

It would not be long. The gambler had ceased his writhings now — was a helpless shape in those lifted arms. Brady stopped by the hitch rack and hoisted him higher.

Gripped by abysmal dread, Ann waited. And, suddenly, tumultuously, joy rushed through her. Connifay, abruptly twisting above him, had brought a spurred boot into Brady's face. With a bellow of rage and pain Brady lurched, lost his footing and went down under Connifay.

Dust rose like smoke, thick and swirling, obscuring. Ann clutched a porch post; and somewhere nearby a voice said: "Damn it all, anyway!" and another voice grumbled, "What the hell's goin' on, Kerley?" Then the two men were up, like shapes in a fog, weaving forward and backward. Brady tried to close, and Connifay struck him once on each temple; and he reeled away, stunned and half blinded, with an animal whimper dribbling out of his throat. Connifay's left hand shot out, caught what was left of Brady's shirt, hauled him around and held him braced there. With tremendous force, with all the fury in him, Connifay's right fist crashed one terrific blow against Joe Brady's askew chin. Brady's head snapped back as if a log had struck it and his toppling body flopped him over the hitch rack, and he lay, supine, in the thick dust beneath it.

Timpas shoved through the crowd, cutting a way with his big, rolling shoulder. Somebody came with a lantern from the stable and held it above the still-unconscious Brady. The crowd pushed forward to have a look at him, to have its word with the man who had bested him; but the gambler ignored them. Watching him, Ann inexplicably felt a strong glow of pride for him; and it came to her that fighting could sometimes be its own full justification, and that even a tinhorn gambler might have an admirable trait or two. Then she saw the Brady girl say something to him, saw her smile at him oddly before she turned away to go to her father.

Connifay wheeled and walked over to Timpas and stood with spread legs and regarded him stilly. Timpas parted his lips in a toothy grin. "For a sick man," he said, "you've got a hell of a damn tough way with your fists."

"Maybe I'm not so sick any more."

"And maybe you weren't never sick in the first place —"

"An' mebbe," Connifay said, flatly and clearly, "you didn't put Brady up to this; but I think you did, and if I find that I'm right you had better get out of this town in a hurry." He looked at Timpas a moment longer, then swung away with a face gone blank and went past the porch with his eyes straight ahead.

Ann turned and looked after him, wishing her brother might have some of his qualities; wishing — But no! She would never wish *that!* The man was a gambler, a tinhorn and killer!

But he stayed in her thoughts just the same . . .

9. Dark Hour

Connifay, with every pounded muscle jangling, with throat rasped raw and his bones like lead, pushed the batwings back and went into the saloon. The lamps had been lighted and their garish flare lay over the room like a lemon blanket, glinting back from the emptied tables and bar. The crowd was gone, still outside, still talking; and the only man in the place, the barman, said: "Here — drink this," and extended a bottle. Connifay passed him without even turning. He climbed the balcony stairs to his cubbyhole, went to its darkness and closed the door.

He got out of the ragged wreck of his clothes, thrust an aching hand in the wash basin's pitcher, found there was water and painstakingly used it. He dried himself off with a piece of his shirt and, with nothing on but his pants, wearily stretched himself out on the blanketless bunk.

He was in for a sleepless night, and knew it. Every inch of him ached; and downstairs the resumed din was reaching its full-blast level of loudness. The cogent sensations of the day's events came back to pummel his mind with questions and, curiously, his longest thoughts were of Timpas.

The man was after something. He was after the Fiddle-Back. He might also be after this entire valley if the range-hog complex lay back of his actions. Whatever his reasons, he had wanted Mark Connifay's name on his pay sheet. This suggested he knew of Mark Connifay's past. Having failed to hire him, Timpas was bending all efforts toward getting rid of him. Connifay had little doubt Timpas had been back of Bannock; back of Bannock and back of Brady, too. Brady hadn't the head to think up such melodrama; somewhere in that attempted tie-up lay a key to Timpas' actions. Had the man been scared he'd hire out to old Kroniac?

It looked mighty like it. Moves such as this were grooved in a pattern, like cards or dice, or the swing of a pistol. There'd been a hollow note in Brady's ranting; not for a second had Connifay swallowed Brady's bellowed wails about his daughter. This was a put-up job and Bella Mae had enjoyed it; several times, riding in, Mark had caught her grinning.

But he gave her her due. She had warned him. In advance she had warned him. At the very start; and tonight, just a while ago — just before he'd come up here, she had taken the trouble to remind him of it. "Remember?" she'd said.

Too well he remembered; but what could there be between her and old Kroniac to give Timpas the idea that marriage — But wait!

Connifay stared fixedly at the pale splotch of the window. There was something . . . He dug into his memory and called up the words she had applied to Kroniac. "Prouder than sheep dip" — she had said the words bitterly.

So there *was* something. Some very good reason for Timpas' opinion that a coupling of Connifay's name with the Brady girl's would keep Mark's name off the Fiddle-Back payroll. And since Kroniac — notwithstanding his dislike of gamblers — had already shown he was willing to hire him, it must be something very fiercely personal.

Mark reared up his head, his shoulders moving impatiently.

It was hot in the room, hot with a trapped heat blown from the desert; and the outside dark pressed against the nailed window with a nameless warning, driving his thoughts down a trail that had grown in these last few years too familiar. The whispering winds were afoot in the hills, old smokes were rising, and it was time for a man to climb into the saddle. The threads of his life had snarled again and trouble — bad trouble — was piling swiftly. Peace was a phantom too quickly fading, and the only thing he could see with certainty was death for himself if he did not leave there.

Yet he knew in his bones that he would not go.

The call, the rank smell of these hills, had got into him — this, and the trust in an old man's eyes. Their hold was on him; and the wistful way the old man had said: "I could use you," was a treasured thing he would not forget. It had been a long, long while since a man had spoken those words, in that tone, to Mark Connifay.

He was trapped by these things — forces he could not have known had he taken Bella Mae's advice and left the country the night he arrived. But mixed with this faint regret was the relief, the certainty, that comes to a man who has found himself. This was the way it had always been, and the way it always would be. The security and comfort of other men's lives were as far from his reach as the gold and green of a rainbow; he was born to trouble, and wherever there were grave-faced men and the sound of women crying, there you would find Mark Connifay.

He must have dozed, he guessed. The room was still dark and night still peered in the window, but the downstairs racket had stopped.

He lay there a moment, lay utterly still, trying to think what it was had awakened him. He did not like the feel of the place, but there seemed nothing wrong that a man could lay hold of.

He pulled up his knees and looked over at the door. The key was a joke. The door couldn't be locked. The room had no chair you could put up against it.

Connifay's hand went out, sought the peg where he'd hung his harness and gun. The harness was there. His exploring fingers touched the butt of his pistol. He took them away, leaving the gun where it was. He guessed, after all, he was just being edgy. The tag-end of the reaction from his fight with Brady.

He sank back on the bunk and then, even yet more than halfway suspicious, came up on an elbow, head tilted, to listen. *There!* It was outside on the balcony; just a sigh of sound so gently soft you could not be sure there had been sound at all.

Connifay was not sure. The vast hush of this country could fool a man into thinking almost anything.

More in irritation than with any real suspicion, Connifay got up off the bed and opened the door.

A gun's cold muzzle was shoved against his stomach.

10. Silver Dollar Joe

There was one thing to do and Connifay did it. His right hand grabbed the gun and his left caught an elbow. Flame sheared whitely through the cowering shadows and there was a roar that rocked the wall boards. Connifay tightened his holds and twisted. The gun fighter screamed and let go of his pistol. Connifay yanked him into the room.

"There's a lamp on the wash stand. Light it."

The scrape of the match showed a tall young man. He had bright, sullen eyes and his hands shook so badly it looked for a while as if he'd break the lamp's chimney; but he got it on finally.

Connifay pushed the door shut. He sat down on the bunk and pulled his boots on, inscrutably watching the would-be killer. The fellow's scared cheeks were a fish-belly white. There was fear in his stare and a wild desperation.

Connifay said: "You look pretty young to be plyin' the killer trade."

The boy locked his teeth to keep them

from chattering and Connifay watched him awhile without speaking. His smooth symmetrical features were almost effeminate in their cameo contours and he did not appear to be more than eighteen; but this in no way tempered Connifay's judgment. In this country many a lad took a man's place much younger and was expected to assume a man's responsibilities.

Connifay said: "Mebbe you better tell me about it."

In some measure the boy seemed to have got hold of himself now. Most of the fright had gone out of his features, and something that was almost defiance looked out of his stare. "Ain't nothin' to tell," he said sullenly.

Connifay said drily: "Tough hombre scowls have never impressed me. You can talk or not — suit yourself. But you're not goin' out of here until you have talked."

"Suits me. I can be comfortable here as I can any other place —"

"I wouldn't be too sure about that. Who put you up to this? Timpas?"

Quick alarm crossed the boy's sallow cheeks. He tried to cover up with a scowl, but Connifay's quiet derision wouldn't let him. His sneer got lost in a sullen flush; and Connifay said: "What has Timpas got on you, kid — what's he holdin' over you?"

The kid jerked his chin up. A quick, surprised look sprang his lids apart widely. He stared a long moment, darkly wondering, trying to read what lay back of the gambler's shrewd question.

Connifay's shoulders lifted impatiently. Irritation got the best of him then. "By grab, boy," he growled, "I wasn't born yesterday! I don't know you from Adam, yet I open the door an' you shove a gun at me! The gun goes off but nobody comes nosin' — Why not? What's holdin' 'em? I can damn well tell you! It's *Ely Timpas!* Start talkin', an' make it straight, or —" He did not bother to finish the threat. He hefted the kid's pistol and got up off the bunk.

The kid backed away, backed till the wall touched the blades of his shoulders. The rims of his eyes showed a strained, edgy care and his knees got to knocking, but Connifay kept coming. That slow, hard tramp of the gambler's boots seemed endowed with an appalling menace. Sweat stood in great drops on the kid's waxen cheeks. The gleam of it beaded his forehead thickly and he quailed, uncontrollably shaking, as Connifay stopped a short arm's length away.

No expression betrayed the gambler's

thoughts. He said with gruff bluntness: "I won't be listenin' much longer."

The kid's eyes rolled and suddenly he cracked, words tumbling out of him raggedly. In the frightened desire to square himself he forgot, for the moment, his fear of Timpas — or, more likely, that fear was lost in the nearer, more certain and therefore more-to-be-propitiated menace of Connifay. He told the whole sordid story. One thing in that flood of words caught Connifay's interest above all others — one name. It made him catch the kid's shirtfront and shake him. "The Fiddle-Back Kroniacs? Mean to tell me you're Miss Ann's brother?"

The kid gulped and ducked his head.

Slowly Connifay's grip relaxed. He had the look of a man in a dream. "Ann's brother . . ." he said, and stepped back, almost jerkily. Then he pulled his big shoulders together; and the streaked edge of a smile that crossed his tight lips held sudden, bitter knowledge. He sighed, shook his head, and sighed once again. "Go on," he said softly.

When the kid had finished, Connifay stood a long moment, silent.

"Did you think he would give you back them notes?"

"He said —"

Connifay's scornful laugh cut him off. "You got any idea where he's keepin' them?"

Young Kroniac shook his head without hope. "Wouldn't make no difference. He won't give 'em up. He told —"

"I expect he did," murmured Connifay drily. "Here's your gun."

"You — you mean I can *go?*"

"The quicker you go the better I'll be suited."

"But —" Tony stared, new worry breaking over his too even features. "What'll I tell Ely?"

"Tell him nothing. Keep clean away from him; let him do the worryin' for a little while —"

"But what about them notes?" It was almost a wail the way young Kroniac said it. "He'll show 'em to —"

"I don't think you need to worry about that." Connifay sat down and pulled off his boots. "You don't want no advice, so I won't give you any. You can forget about Timpas. He is my affair now and I will take care of him."

Tony finally let out a long breath relievedly. He shifted his weight, looked at Connifay curiously. "It's funny," he said finally with a boy's embarrassment. "I come up here to kill you. I — you — well, I — I just want to say I'm —"

"Forget it," said Connifay gruffly. He turned down the lamp's wick. "Good night, kid."

In the Single Cinch office of the syndicate, Timpas, still cursing the hated gambler who had publicly humbled him twice in as many days, took some papers from his safe and swung the big door shut. Not bothering to lock it, he dumped the papers onto his desk and dropped heavily into the swivel chair back of it. He sat for a long time unmoving, bitterly scowling, staring off into space, some premonition riding him strongly, disturbing the plans he would have shaped for Connifay's swift undoing. Doom seemed to lurk in the room's gathered shadows, in the waterfall patter of the town's dusty foliage; doom swift and sure unless he found some way to throttle that gambler — to drive the man out or get the best of him.

"By Gawd," Timpas said, "I *will* get the best of him! No man can use me like that son has and not get paid back for it! *No* man!" And the way he clubbed the desk with his fist made the frames of the yonder windows rattle.

Nothing should stand in the way of this thing he had set his heart on. He would go on as he had planned, turning one set of ranchmen against another, big men against little, with pillage and ambush and arson for hole-cards, till the country's creeks ran red with blood and all this high hill region was thrown to the wolves of chaos!

And why not?

Here was this vast stretch of country, which could so easily have been made a green paradise, lying forgotten, unknown and uncared for, a hideout for rustlers and fly-by-night outlaws because of the hide-bound shortsightedness of the witless fools who controlled it. And who would be hurt by his plans for its betterment? Fools, crooks and riffraff — trash whose loss would be a boon to the country. Why should he have any thought for them? He did not, and would not. They were thieves anyway, and some bragged of it. So let them watch out; he would show them thievery that would pull their guts out. As for Connifay — young Tony Kroniac would take care of *him*.

In a considerably better frame of mind Timpas lighted the lamp.

Going back to his desk, he leafed through the papers he had got from the safe. He laid out a couple and, when he was through, looked them over carefully, paying close heed to the writing, detailedly scanning the signatures. Then he took a printed sheet from the pile, dipped pen in ink and with a thin little smile filled in the form's blanks. And signed it.

Afterwards he sat awhile regarding the place where Jackson had dropped. The man was buried, without bother to coroner or clergy. This country had no ceremony to waste on the passing of a cinch ring expert. Timpas had scribbled a brief note to the sheriff. Nothing more was necessary.

Leaning back in the chair, he stretched his long legs, peeled the wrappings from another packet of his black cigars and lit one, puffing enjoyably. Jackson's passing was another small mile on the Timpas path to empire.

Gravel crunched in the night outside and a faint smile edged Timpas' arrogant lips. Knowing that step, he did not turn when the man came in; he let the man come around to face him. He said, knowing how it would gall the man: "Back for more orders, Fargo?"

Fargo, with his back to the wall, stood and stared at Timpas woodenly. He had a power — the power of silence and an Indian-like impassivity; it had, in fact, been frequently hinted that some of his folks wore moccasins. He was a hard, still man whom few cared to cross. He had suited Timpas well in the past; but now, as he studied the man's unfathomable glance, doubts rose in the mind of the Wet Moon boss. Unpleasant memories rolled across his roan cheeks and he said gratingly, "What were you doing with Hackberry's crew the night that gambler killed Bannock?"

Fargo said: "The syndicate buys my workin' hours. How I spend the rest of my time —"

"When I hire a man, I hire every minute of his time — understand?"

Fargo's unwinking eyes watched Timpas but he did not open his mouth to speak. He was a man who answered to nothing but the whip; he could not understand softness, and Timpas was halfway out of his chair before he said: "Yeah," reluctantly.

"Then remember it."

Timpas' deep, wide chest was filled with turbulence and there was hate and rage in his willful stare, but he kept his desires in abeyance. His score with Fargo could wait.

He picked up the printed form he'd filled out and pushed it across the desk, examined his purse and extracted some silver. "This is a quit-claim deed to the Jackson place. I want it taken to Mesilla and recorded in my name. Do it yourself and get started right now."

Something sly looked out of the range boss' eyes. "Guess them Eastern owners of yours —"

"Get your horse an' do what I say!" Timpas snarled.

Mark Connifay lay awake on his bunk long after young Kroniac's limping departure. His bruised throat ached with a throbbing misery and his muscles felt as if they'd been scraped with a hoe. Twice, while he lay there thinking, he had heard hoofbeats in the street below. The first had heralded an arrival, but the second — this new sound beating up now — told of a rider departing in a hurry. A solitary horseman traveling southeast. Connifay wondered who had gone off at that hour; and next thing he knew it was morning. Not early morning, either. The sun was up and it was already warm. A cowbird chirped in the scrub oak yonder.

Mark pulled on his boots and tramped to the wash stand. There was still a bit of water in the crockery pitcher, and he felt a little better after washing his face. He had slept in his pants and they were criss-crossed with creases. He gave the remains of his shirt a wry smile, picked up the wreck of his coat and got into it, fastening the one button Brady had left. He was at the door when he remembered his gun. He went back and got it, thrusting it into his pocket.

If feelings were any criterion, he must look like the wrath of God, he thought. He would have to buy a new outfit.

He moved out on the balcony and was on the stairs, at the turn where they dropped to the barroom, when a burst of laughter from down below came up to stop him like a roughlock brake.

He stood quite still, listening into the silence, hearing the eager resumption of talk through the harsh lift of memories that ran through his head. He went down three more steps and stopped, his glance raking the men gathered round the bar. The muscles of his long lips tightened a little. That was all.

He went on down the stairs with an even step and was almost at the bottom when one of the group at the bar looked around and saw him. The man stared with wide eyes and stood as though frozen. Then color faintly stained his cheeks and his elbow nudged the man beside him. When this man saw Connifay his eyes went lean and black with hate.

There was no expression on Connifay's face as he stepped off the stairs and came to the bar.

"Hello, Joe," he said.

11. Complications

There was an ominous vacuity in the gaze of the Texas sheriff; but as Connifay stopped before him his eyes took on a glitter and his shoulder muscles ripped with a kind of grim repression.

"I'm goin' —" he said, peeling back his lips; and stopped like that with his stare gone wide and uncertain. He'd had violent notions but now they were gone, dissolved in the sweat that broke out on his brow. Something read in the gambler's stare had corroded his will, had locked his muscles and the nerves that governed them.

The quiet piled up, became insupportable.

"Well," said Connifay, "what are you waitin' for?"

The dark scowling stares that he got from his deputies flushed the sheriff's cheeks with anger. But he had no mind to make another mistake. He took his hand away from his gun and showed his teeth in a sneering grimace. "You can sure rile a man — I'll give you that. But it's no kind of use, Mark; you're wastin' your talent. We didn't come here for you an' we're not lookin' for you. I run you out of Texas an' —"

"Shucks," drawled Connifay, coolly easy. "You ain't really believin' such foolishness, are you? Mebbe I better freshen up your memory —"

"Never mind wastin' sweat thinkin' up more lies. Long's you keep out of Texas the law will be satisfied."

"Why, Joe, that's handsome. Law must of had a new deal since I left. Them fair words includin' your own score, too?"

There was a cadence in the gambler's tone that reddened the sheriff's cheeks again, and he ground out hotly: "I'll take care of that —"

"But not around here, Joe. There ain't enough rabbit brush screenin' the boulders."

Connifay laughed as he stepped through the batwings.

Tony Kroniac, heading for home through the starlit night, knew a new sense of freedom. All the conduits of his blood sang an anthem of elation as he thought of the stranger and the stranger's promise. "You can forget about Timpas. He is my

111

affair now and I will take care of him," the gambler had said. And, looking into the man's cold eyes, Tony had felt that he would do just that; do it well and efficiently and, very probably, finally.

But fear, he found, was not a thing easily thrust aside. His mercurial temperament, swayed by the expensive knowledge he had gained of Timpas, was no sufficient grapple by which to hang onto trust, and the longer he rode the more uneasy he became. Doubts and suspicions leered back from the shadows; and he pulled up suddenly, amazed at his credulity.

Why should this Connifay bother to help him? Who *was* the man anyway? A saddle-blanket gambler from somewhere in Texas who had probably never heard of him before tonight! Why should the man go out of his way to help a fellow who had tried to kill him?

He wouldn't, of course — that was plain enough now. Tony cursed himself for a fool. All that gambler's fine talk had been a ruse, designed to get Tony out of the place. He had never intended doing anything for Tony. If he got those IOU's at all, it would be for his own use.

It never occurred to young Kroniac to wonder to what use the gambler could put them. He had spent too many nights worrying over them to see them as representing in another's hands anything save unqualified disaster to himself.

With cold sweat on his cheeks, Tony conjured countless fearful outcomes to this night's business.

He reined up sharply with a startled whistle. That safe! Why hadn't he thought of it sooner? All his worries, all those sleepless nights rose up to mock and jeer at him. What a fool he had been to think himself helpless. All he had to do was open that safe, pick up his paper and clear out with it. It wouldn't be robbery; all he'd be doing would be getting back his own. He could thumb his nose at Ely then!

He whirled his horse with his spurs brightly flashing. He would get those notes, himself, before morning.

Buffalo Grote, the Kroniac range boss, shoving into the saloon on the heels of Connifay's exit, peered curiously at the crew by the bar. He gave the three strangers a taciturn interest, waved two fingers at the bartender and said to the houseman, Dorado Stoggins:

"Found out where them cattle been goin'. Whoa Jackson, the rimfire whistle tick, has been makin' himself a business out of 'em! Been runnin' 'em across the border, by grab — sellin' 'em off just like he owned 'em. You heard about Timpas killin' him las' night? Well —"

Stoggins, without any interest in the Fiddle-Back cattle, said: "These gents been inquirin' the way to your outfit. Meet Buffalo Grote, gents. He's Kroniac's range boss."

Silver Dollar looked Grote over uncharitably. "I'm a relative of Kroniac; these fellows are friends of mine. We'd like to —"

"Sure," Grote said. "Glad to know you. Be startin' right away. Just as quick's I git this cussed alkali . . ."

Tony's mad pace did not last overlong. Disturbing thoughts crept into his mind and, nervously, he slowed his horse the better to consider them. There were a lot of risks in this venture that he had not seen at the notion's first blush. He was still of a mind to break open Timpas' safe — but what if the Wet Moon boss should catch him? What if Timpas should come tramping in just as he was tucking those notes in his pocket!

Cold fingers touched Tony's spine at the thought; cold sweat made his neck clammy,

114

moistened the scowl on his forehead, and he was of half a mind to swing round and go home. But memory of Timpas' threat stiffened him. Tomorrow noon, unless prevented, Timpas would take those IOU's to his father. The prospect of his father's wrath perturbed Tony more than his fears of Timpas. Even death, he thought, would be preferable to that.

Time was against him. There were not two hours between himself and dawn when across the sentinel spikes of yucca he caught the lights of the Cap and Ball.

With pounding heart he whirled from the trail. A flutter of hoofs drummed up from the hardpan. Someone was coming from town like a mallet. Through the spectral moonlight Tony saw the man, low in his saddle, bright spurs flashing, cutting southeast toward the ghostly pass that led through the Organs toward distant Texas.

Who was it? Connifay? Was the tinhorn quitting the country? Getting out at last — getting run out perhaps? With all his heart Tony fervently hoped so. With each recurrent vision of the Texan, he had known new fears, new risks, new terrors. It was astounding what that man's eyes could do! He'd been a fool to tell Connifay what hold Timpas had on him!

Through the screening brush Tony's eyes went narrow. A baffled wonder crept into their glint. The man was not Connifay. A cow-puncher! — you could see the flutter of the scarf at his neck — the curly-brimmed Stetson — the windbatted flaps of his cowhide vest.

Gad! It was Fargo! The Wet Moon range boss! By all that was holy, where was *he* off to? At this time of night! At such headlong speed!

What kind of errand would Timpas be having that would take his foreman — Or was it Fargo's business that was lashing that horse? But no; a man's every business belonged to Timpas when his name was down on Timpas' pay sheet. Timpas' money bought *all* your time, and you'd damn well give it if you knew what was good for you!

Tony stayed in the oak brush a considerable while trying to worry dark meaning into Fargo's departure. That its meaning *was* dark he had no doubt at all. Both the hour and the speed were conducive to mystery, and it was in Tony's mind that it might touch on himself. Mesilla lay on that trail Fargo'd taken. Mesilla was the only town of size in that country — the last nebulous outpost of constituted law; it was there that the sheriff hung up his hat, and there that the circuit court convened when it suited the judge and the judge's affairs spared him.

Tony mused and muttered to the outskirts of town, and his badgered mind was further harried when he saw the huddle of horse shapes etched in the lights of the Cap and Ball.

He climbed from the saddle in a clump of squat cedar where the saloon's dim lamps did not reach through the gloom. More mystery! He was fretfully convinced those would not be the broncs of any valley outfit, for none were paid off at this time of the month. They must, therefore, be the mounts of strangers, and Tony, like Grote, was suspicious of strangers. Timpas had, to his knowledge, hired eighteen strangers in the past thirty days.

Was Timpas the magnet that drew them there? If so, to what purpose? What was the man up to and what did he want with these strangers he hired? Where did they go when they left with his blessing? They were not at the Wet Moon — Tony had checked on that, had lain on the rimrock for two solid days watching Timpas' home outfit with meticulous care.

Disgruntled, he shrugged and walked

out of the cedars, striking off to the left to round the dark warehouse. He rounded it, stopped; stopped and stared, softly swearing.

There was a lamp burning brightly in Timpas' office.

12. "They Blowed Their Lights Plumb Out!"

On the night following Connifay's clash with Tony, Ann Kroniac sat in the Fiddle-Back ranch house with an open book lying forgotten in her lap. It was a good book, too — one read many times, but just now unpalatable. Life, which to her had always been a straight line, had suddenly become complex and bewildering.

Her father was worried. Not that he had said so or consciously shown it. Ann had her woman's ways of knowing; and she was sure his worry had nothing to do with her brother's inexplicable absence.

She knew intuitively it was the Fiddle-Back that was bothering him; this great ranch of theirs that had ever given him so much pride, so much satisfaction. It was his keenest interest, a thing he had shaped and nourished as a heritage for his children; its iron was his coat of arms, its life *his* life, inseparably.

Ann knew its affairs were in bad shape,

had grown steadily worse in the past month or so. She suspected Ely Timpas somehow, but would not put this hunch to words, knowing her father's esteem for the man.

She had always found Timpas agreeable, in marked contrast to the other men of this country who made no pretense of liking her father. He was traveled, could talk intelligently; his whimsical tales of the earth's far places both amazed and delighted her. Big he was — big in mind and body; a robust figure of strapping manhood, efficient and confident, compellingly attractive — by far the handsomest man in the Organs. His Eastern clothes, which on anyone else would have appeared ridiculous, he wore with a graceful ease that was truly magnificent. She guessed his age as from thirty-five to forty; not by his looks, but because of his travels and mentioned experience. In appearance he looked not a day over thirty, showing all youth's fire, quick temper and arrogance.

But though she felt strongly attracted to the man, Ann did not wholly trust Ely Timpas. Big, vital, magnetic as the man undeniably was, there were times when his clipped urbanity left her silent and thoughtful, times when his talk struck a wrong note somehow and his dark, swiftly measuring glance and amused smile aroused doubts — when the man's blatant egotism seemed almost insufferable; and at such times she wondered if he were all he appeared to be. Veiled though it was, she sensed a hard streak in him, an obsidian core that could be implacably ruthless. He would not, she thought, be a good man to cross.

But it was her father who especially held Ann's thoughts tonight. The ranch was short-handed and Grote, the Fiddle-Back range boss, she felt certain was either incompetent or crooked. She could see no excuse for keeping the men around headquarters, as Grote had been doing, when rustlers were working the hills like locusts. Not a day went past without some new tale of outrage. She had spoken of Grote to her father, but he had waved the matter aside impatiently. "God's blood girl!" he'd said. "Where would I dig up another boss now?" No, the matter went deeper than rustling.

Someone — Ann felt intensely sure of this — was out to smash the Fiddle-Back; out to take their ranch over.

Thought of the stranger came to her then, that hard-fisted gambler — that tinhorn trickster from Texas. She was resolutely certain she did not like him. He was a cheap, card-sharping crook who was ever ready to grab for a gun when the play went not to his liking — she had heard all about him from her uncle. Silver Dollar had known him well in the bloody days of the Smith's Crossing feud; and Silver Dollar's description of him had left out nothing worth mentioning. And she had seen for herself what a brawler he was. That she had for a moment admired him was beside the point entirely. That had been due to excitement; to the primitive lusts unloosed by the savage spectacle she had witnessed from the porch of the general store. She was ashamed of herself for having watched it, for the unguessed urges it had revealed in her, for the taint of the disloyal thoughts it had roused.

She would not think of it, nor of Connifay.

She picked up her book, determined to get the man out of mind. Watching him in town last night, she had thought —

With a grimace Ann focused her mind on the printed page; and at that moment someone knocked on the door. It startled her, for she had heard no sound of an approaching horse, no hollow *whoom* from the plank bridge yonder. It was probably

Grote come to see her father about something pertaining to the running of the ranch. She laid down her book, wondering where her father had gone after supper.

She glanced at the clock; it was almost eleven! Her father had been riding old Strawberry. Could something have happened — had he met with an accident? A premonition of disaster touched her heart with cold fingers. In a tremble of fright she pulled open the door. The breath caught in her throat.

"You!"

Connifay smiled.

Seen in that refracted light, his eyes were the color of smoky sage. Serene, unabashed, they met Ann Kroniac's straightly as he stood there whimsically facing her. He did not speak immediately and she thought she read something derisive in his look, as though he had judged her and found her wanting. She had sensed the same impertinence yesterday when he'd doffed his beaver with that brazen bow; and, as then, she grew furiously angry.

But she would not show it; she would not give him that satisfaction.

"Well?"

"Got your quirt around handy?" Though

123

he swung his head for a look at the bunkhouse, she caught the burred edge of his mockery and color stained the slants of her cheeks. Then his eyes were back and he was saying casually: "If your brother's here I'd like a word with him."

"I doubt if he'd be interested in the word of a gambler."

"Perhaps," he said coolly, "you'd better call him."

She said quickly: "What do you want with him?"

"I'm not going to shoot him, if that's what's eatin' you. He asked me to do something and —"

"I don't believe you! I doubt if you even know my brother."

"I expect your brother is the best judge of that." He grinned at the quick way she lifted her chin. Then the smile went off his face and he said: "I'll be on my way sooner if you'll call him, ma'am."

"He's not here."

"Not here!" He showed surprise. His eyes, she thought, held an odd, strained look. "When do you expect him?"

"I don't know." She said impatiently: "Can't you give me the message?"

He stood there, silent, appearing to consider. He was dressed like a cowman now, she saw. But clothes could not change what was in a man's blood, or his past, or the hard, cruel ways of his life. These were the things which set him apart; these, and his deadly way with a gun.

Memories rose to confuse and unsettle her. She saw the gambler's glance quicken. Her cheeks felt hot. She was surprised at the tact that took his glance away. She saw him then as a lonely man with a depth of feeling and perception not to be looked for in one of his calling.

Some measure of her anger drained away and she spoke with an impulsiveness that afterwards astonished her. "Why do you stay here where everyone hates you?"

He looked at her queerly. "Are you sure you want me to tell you that?"

Some half sensed significance in his odd, tight tone unsettled and startled her. She fell back, at once wide-eyed and frightened. All the bitterness, all the savage restraint of his words cut into her, twisting her, swaying her, shaking and pounding her, blasting away all her firm resolves, battering fiercely her will's last barrier. He could not know, must *never* know, how terribly she was drawn to him; how desperately she was fighting to regain her self-control.

She saw his head come up suddenly, saw

him wheel to his horse with a hollow laugh. Watched him climb to the saddle with stiff cheeks, barely pausing to toss something onto the porch planks.

She stood with both hands whitely clenched on the door frame. But pride was the barrier that had stood against him, and pride would not let her call to him now. Stricken she stood there, numbly listening to the sound of his going grown dim with distance. Long after it faded she was still there listening.

The night was bright but she could not see.

The sun was a dying blaze redly lighting the Sierra Cahalos when Grote and his party rode up to the line camp. Jawbone's dolorous voice drifted in as he drearily rounded the bedded beef. Studhoss hunkered by a cookfire. "How the hell many times do you eat?" the range boss dyspeptically growled at him.

"I eat," Studhoss said, "when I git a chancet. An' if you don't like it you can give me my time."

Grote glowered a moment and went into the cabin.

Jawbone's lament drifted back from the cattle:

126

"The summer sun was settin',
    It felled with lingerin' ray
Through the gnarled limbs of a forest
    Where a wounded Ranger lay.
In the shade of blue palmetter,
    Beneath the blaze o' sky
Far off from his loved Texas
    We had laid down to die."

Grote came over to the fire. "Chuck in some more of that beef an' mix up a batch of biscuit. That's the Ol' Man's brother-in-law an' a coupla his friends from Texas."

Studhoss gave the strangers a laconic glance and went on with his chuck fixing. When the coffee was ready Grote got himself a cupful and a pan of beef from the skillet. With a mouth crammed full, he told the guests: "Any you fellas hungry, better grab you some while she's goin'."

Studhoss filled the skillet with batter. Grote said: "Never mind shakin' in that soda. Makes me yeller —"

"You allus was yeller," Studhoss spat. "Don't blame it onto my cookin'."

Ann, by the living room table, stood a long time looking at the envelope Connifay had flung on the porch. No marks of any kind were on it, but she guessed it was this he had come to give Tony. Even so, there really was no reason why she should not open it. This was the second night of Tony's absence and there might be something contained in this note that she would better act on. She glanced again at the clock and found it was but fifteen minutes till midnight.

The strange uneasiness that had gripped her grew, filling her mind with morbid fancies, coloring her thoughts with the hues of doom. She went to a window, moved across to the door, the emotions roused by Connifay's visit still plaguing her with thoughts she would not let herself think.

She pulled on her gloves, peeled them off impatiently. She dared not leave the house. She tried to calm herself with commonplace things — by telling herself that a horseman as experienced as her father could not possibly have met with harm while he had old Strawberry under the saddle. He was all right; detained on business; had probably gone to town after supper. Perhaps he had gone to see Ely Timpas.

Her worried glance went round the room, each familiar thing touched reviving some forgotten memory. She turned abruptly and came back to the table. Picking up the gambler's envelope, she tore it open, upended and shook it. Slips of paper torn from some rider's tally book cascaded like snow-flakes across the dark gleam of the table. Little slips that were all of a pattern, all geared to the scrawl of Tony's writing.

She read one — stiffened. Electrified, she picked up another, another and still another. They were all the same, all IOU's; only the sums scribbled on them were different.

Card table debts!

There could be no other explanation possible.

Ann's cheeks lost color as she thought of her father and what he might do should he ever discover this. His rage — She shied from the thought as from a white-hot iron. His hatred of gambling was almost a mania. His father had been a wealthy planter till the lust for card tables had finally ruined him. He had gone to the out-house one night and shot himself, leaving his son a debt it had taken him twenty-five years to be rid of. He'd been forty-three when he'd founded the Fiddle-Back; and no longer ago than only last summer he had told young Tony: "Next time you sit down to a card table, boy, don't bother getting up to come home again."

It was this knowledge which had made it so startling, so hard to believe, that her father could actually have offered Connifay a job. It was a desperate commentary . . .

Feverishly she bent, transcribing figures, setting them down in a ragged column; and when she had them all she totaled them and was appalled at their enormous sum.

What awful price had Tony paid to clear this debt with the Smith's Crossing gambler?

The papers fell from her trembling fingers; she caught at the table to brace herself. Some things were plain to her now.

She shuddered as one coming out of a nightmare, seeing again the dark mocking glint of Connifay's stare as he wheeled off the porch with that tight, bitter laughter.

There was tumult in her. Each strangled breath honed conviction sharper. The flogging pulse of hoof sound roused her. Quick it was, and somehow frantic, filling the night like a prelude to doom.

Those notes! She must hide them!

She caught them up and with a desperate haste thrust them into her blouse and hurried hallward. She shrank from the door; summoned courage — pulled it open. Through a curtain of dust she saw the stopped horses. Grote's bull voice slammed across the yard: "Git your father! Git him out here — *quick!*"

"He isn't —"

"Git that hump-footed brother of yours out here then!"

Ann cried, frightened: "He hasn't come back yet," and was dimly aware of stumbling toward them. There were only two riders. Through the resettling dust they were eying each other.

Ann fought to control the weakness that seemed to be turning her blood into water. "Buffalo!" she called out. "Please — what is it?"

The range boss hesitated, twisted his hat and looked at the other man. This second rider spoke then, and with an unbounded sense of relief Ann heard the strong, welcome voice of her Uncle Joe. "This is Silver, Ann. Brace yourself, girl; this news is bad. Rustlers have stripped the Fiddle-Back range, stampeded the beef and —"

"We was damn lucky to git clear," Grote growled. "Musta been twenty-thirty of 'em. They got Jawbone, Studhoss, two gents what come with your uncle —"

"Got them?" Ann hardly recognized that

faint voice as hers. "You — you mean the raiders took —"

"Took hell!" Grote snarled. *"They blowed their lights plumb out!"*

13. Caught!

When Tony saw the light in Timpas' office he knew defeat. He had been prepared to break a safe in an empty building; he was not at all prepared to bend a gun on a man like Timpas. The Wet Moon boss was the very last man he wanted to see at that moment. He backed precipitantly away, getting his horse and riding out into the greasewood, sweatingly thankful he had not been seen.

All that day he remained concealed in the creosote brush that fringed the Jornada, a prey to hunger and indecision, not daring to show himself in the daylight lest some spy of Timpas see and report him. His mind was a cauldron of seething fancies; he tortured himself with visions of Timpas taking those notes to his father at the Fiddle-Back, with other calamities even more weird. All day he lay there, clammy with the sweat of his fears and fancies, lacking the mental stature to see that his precious notes were important to Timpas only so long as they were kept where they were and *away* from where he had threatened to take them. Ann's brother was not entirely a fool; he was weak and vacillating, unfitted by nature to hold a man's place in that country.

He seemed, oddly enough, with the descent of the sun to gather courage; or perhaps his subsequent movements were actuated by that recklessness which is born of despair — a last frantic gesture against glimpsed futility.

When night came down to hide his travel he mounted his horse and circled the town, approaching Timpas' office much as he'd done the previous night, only this time when he walked round the warehouse he had his horse with him. As before, there was a lamp's illumination outlining the shape of the blanket-hung window.

He was not surprised. It was still pretty early and, after having waited all day, a few more hours' delay meant little to him. He drew the horse back into the brush and sat down to wait till Timpas should leave the place. The late-rising moon was a high silver ball when the lamp winked out and he saw Ely Timpas tramp off toward the saloon.

Now to find if the notes were still round there or if Timpas had taken them out to the Fiddle-Back. Perhaps — But Tony would not let himself think that big Timpas might have them stowed in his pocket.

Keeping as much in the shadows as the terrain made possible, Tony crept forward and tried the door. The unexpected discovery that it had not been locked threatened again to unnerve him. He thought of traps, of alarms — wild dangers; backed fearfully off and went round to the back. He tried the window; it slid up quietly. He crouched there, nervous. He licked his cracked lips and held aside an edge of the blanket. No foreign sound disturbed the stillness; there was no sound of all but his own rasping breathing.

He laughed with a sudden access of relief. He thrust a leg swiftly over the sill and, a moment later, was passing Timpas' desk. That end of the room was black with pooled shadows, and his outstretched, wavering hand stopped suddenly, frenziedly, against cold metal. He almost shrieked, so great was his terror; and when he realized it was only the iron of the safe the resultant relief very nearly unhinged him. He leaned weak and trembling against the wall, and was that way, panting, half sick with excitement, when he heard the creak of a door being opened.

He whirled like a cat.

It *was!* It was *this* door!

Without thought he dived for the one open window, going cleanly through, going headlong into a taut, grunting body whose steel-trap arms locked round him fiercely.

A husky shout nearly broke his eardrums: "I got him, Ely! Git a light up quick!"

Tony knew that whisky-blurred voice. It belonged to the gun-runner — Bella Mae's father.

Timpas held up the lamp he'd got lighted. Tony's eyes goggled.

The safe stood open, stood open and empty. Its papers were scattered all over the floor.

Connifay pulled up his horse and stared.

Since leaving the Fiddle-Back his thoughts had not been pleasant; he'd had a hard time cutting loose of them. He wiped sweaty palms on the wings of his chaps with three years' care and vigilance breaking through the clutch of his thinking. There was a rider yonder trying to head him off, and it might be smart to let him have his way. Smart or not, Mark Connifay was in a mood to welcome trouble.

He walked his horse down the rim of the slope. The faraway lights of town flickered dimly. Off to the left the crash of breaking brush proclaimed the haste of a headlong progress. One thought dug into Connifay then. There was no security in that country. No law but the fear each man packed in his holster.

The rider broke from the trees, and yanked his horse to a slithering stop on its haunches. Connifay's look went inscrutably narrow. This was no man. It was Bela Mae Brady.

"Thank heaven!" she cried. Her voice was husky. "I thought it was you but I couldn't be sure. I was going to the Fiddle-Back . . ."

She was in the grip of some nervous excitement. It showed in the deep rise and fall of her breathing, in the quick frightened way her words ran together. She was watching him queerly, he thought — almost desperately. "You'll do me a favor, Mark, won't you?"

"A favor?"

"Oh, I know what you're thinking!" She shook her head fiercely. "You're wrong — this is straight, Mark — I swear it is! I wouldn't ask for myself — But there's nobody else I could go to, but Kroniac. Don't make me, Mark — please!"

She seemed frantic, beside herself.

Connifay said: "What is it you want me to do?"

"Stop them — you've *got* to! It — it's Tony — young Kroniac!"

"Thought you had no use for that tribe."

"I ain't! I hate them! But —" She tossed the dark curls out of her eyes. She put out a hand and her breath quickened raggedly. "My father'd go a mighty far piece to do a Kroniac a meanness. Ely's madder than hops and my father's been with him — been drinkin' all day. They been cookin' up something. It's to do with Tony —"

"I still don't see —"

"They figure to trap him tonight. Over in Ely's office — don't ask me how — I don't know. But I know my father. He'll *kill* that kid!"

Connifay looked at her skeptically. Brady might indeed have it in for the Kroniacs, but it seemed unlikely he'd go as far as murder. Bella Mae was overwrought, was imagining things. Either that, or —

He said: "Why should you think *I* care what happens to him?" and was instantly, somberly, displeased with himself. He saw her wince, draw back from him. There was strain in her voice.

"You — you won't help me . . ."

He held silent, considering. He did not

138

trust the sound of her story. She was lying or else she was holding something back from him. He had no wish to pry into her secrets. He had no wish to be tricked again, either. He had sampled enough of the Brady playfulness.

It was hard in that light to guess her expression; the moon's silver had a way of changing values. He could not read what was in her eyes.

"If you want to tell me the truth —"

"Truth! Do you think I want to see the boy *killed?*"

"I think there's something in the back of your head —"

"You fool!" She lifted both arms as though she would strike him. "You're like all the rest of the men around here — dogs!" she cried fiercely. "Mad dogs that are born to raise hell!"

Connifay, moodily watching her, thought again how rich this girl was in the things for which the Lord had fashioned a woman . . . the beginning and end of all man's contrivings . . .

"I think," he said tiredly, "I'll say good night, ma'am," and at once turned his horse away into the brush.

Tony, facing Timpas and Brady in the office, licked dry lips and could find no words. Timpas' eyes blazed sullen anger but Brady's look was purely wicked. He spoke no words but his mouth was driveling like the jowls of a wolf. Tony remembered, wincing, how he'd tried to break free, how Brady had dropped him with one clout of a gun barrel. They had him flopped in a chair now, aching and nauseated, and the trickle of water leaking off his chin gave the explanation of how they'd brought him to.

He looked at the gun-runner; looked away quickly. He put a hand to his head and his shaking fingers came away sticky.

"Going to talk?" Timpas smiled.

Tony shivered and stared about wildly.

"Come on," Brady wheedled. "Leave me hit 'im, Ely."

"He'll talk," Timpas said, "if he knows what's good for him. How about it, Humpfoot? You took them notes. Now what did you do with them?"

"I never —"

"Look," Brady said, holding out a fist. And when Tony looked Brady hit him, smashing him, chair and all, over backwards.

Brady reached down then and dragged him erect, held him against the wall by his shirtfront. Timpas said, "What did you do with those IOU's?" and Brady balled up a fist again, hopefully.

Tony's cheeks went white as the bleached wood around him. His goggling eyes stared at Brady's fist. "I — I —"

"Hurry up," Timpas said, "I've other business to tend besides yours. You took those notes. I mean to know what you did with them."

Tony said in a sudden access of fear: "You got to believe me, Ely — As God's my witness I ain't laid eyes on them! I ain't! I swear it! I come here to get them, but — but —"

Timpas looked at Brady. Brady looked at his fist.

Tony's knees got to shaking and only the gun-runner's grip on his shirt kept him upright. Timpas bit the end off a black cigar and a kind of dry humor was in the curl of his lips. He said, watching Tony: "Ever had any practice with a blacksnake, Joe?"

"Git yore whip an' watch me!" Brady grinned.

Tony sagged in his grip, but the gun-runner's knee brought him screaming upright.

Brady's laugh fell suddenly off his lips. He let Tony drop and went three steps backward; that sound pulling Timpas' shoulders round from where he bent above the drawer of his desk. His widened stare followed Brady's look to the long, still shape that stood in the doorway.

14. The Fox and the Wolf

Connifay's face was bone and skin with no expression on it.

Timpas' cheeks were pounded putty, and Tony, watching wide-eyed, breathless, knew a mighty surge of exultation. Brady stood with his gold teeth showing, mouth stretched awry in a scream that had frozen long before it could reach his throat.

"Get on your horse, kid, an' get the hell out of here."

Tony's spurs rasped sound from the rough pine flooring.

No one moved, no one spoke till he'd gone through the window. Connifay then began to walk toward Brady. You could see Brady's muscles leap and stiffen. A stifled breath crept out of his throat. One hand plunged down and closed round his gun butt, was starting to lift when the gambler's fist struck him.

The sound was like a dry stick snapping. Brady's head slammed into the wall and Brady's shape went down it, groaning.

"Next time I come after you," Connifay

said, "it'll be with a gun."

His chilled steel gaze swung around, raked Timpas.

Ely Timpas licked dry lips.

The place was so quiet you could hear the leaves rattle as a vagrant breeze touched the trees outside.

Mark Connifay said: "You didn't believe me, did you, when I said you had better get out of this town?"

A tremor ran through Timpas' burly frame. There was sweat on his cheeks and his eyes were like agate.

"I'm *tellin'* you now," murmured Connifay bleakly. "Get out — do you hear me? Get out and stay out."

" 'Cause you'll do what if I don't?" Timpas sneered.

"You had better not wait to find out."

Tony, eating breakfast in the Fiddle-Back mess shack next morning with his father, his uncle and the range boss, Grote, still burned with the fever of last night's excitement. He had just finished telling them of Connifay's clash with Brady and Timpas; he had not, however, mentioned the cause of that clash, letting them imagine it to be some aftermath of the gambler's earlier run-in with Brady.

Silver Dollar's lips curled. The cheeks of the range boss were schooled to blankness. Only Andre Kroniac showed a plain interest. "What do you know about him, Silver?"

Their Texas relative sneered, shrugging his shoulders. "He's a four-flushin' bluffer. Noisier'n hell on cartwheels — got a gun-barrel stare that would give a man nightmares. But pin him right down an' what've you got? No more sand'n you could put in a woman's thimble. Take my advice an' don't waste your time thinkin' of him."

"We're goin' to need men bad —"

"Men, yes; but —"

"What have you got against the fellow, Silver? Aside from that water fight. Got anything against him personally?"

"If I had, do you s'pose he'd still be livin'?" The Texan's look was irritable; belligerence stared from the twist of his scowl. "He cost me a lot of money in that fight —"

"But aside from that fight?" persisted Kroniac.

"Aside from that," Silver growled reluctantly, "I got nothin' against him but what any right-minded man would have towards a back-drillin' killer. He's the same breed o' cats as the rest of these gunslicks —"

Old Andre brushed that aside impatiently.

"What I'm tryin' to get at is the truth of the man. I can get that kind of hogwash off anybody; I know his rep — what I want is what's back of it."

"How do you mean 'back of it'?"

"Give me a few unvarnished details. Who has he killed? When, why an' how did he kill 'em? How does it —"

Silver Dollar's bench scraped back. "If you're goin' to take up with gamblers —"

Ann, coming in from the cook shack with another plate of food, said: "What kind of a gambler is he, Silver?"

"Is there more than one kind?"

"Is he just a tinhorn or a real high roller — is he *crooked?*"

Silver looked from one to another of them, his glance growing darker and darker. "By grab," he said at last, looking at Kroniac, "I been under the notion you couldn't *abide* gamblers. Mebbe I've got the wrong pew here. Mebbe you ain't wantin' my —"

"Sit down," Kroniac said, "an' talk sensible. This ain't no time for quibblin', Silver — we're goin' to need all the help we can get. Answer the girl; is he straight or crooked?"

"Oh, he's straight enough, far's his gamblin' goes —"

"Holdin' a Texas warrant for him, are you?"

"No, I ain't got no warrant, but if you're thinkin' to hire him you're plain damn crazy!"

"I always been called that," Old Andre chuckled, and resumed his eating with a livelier appetite.

Two afternoons later Connifay rode into the Currycomb ranch yard. There was no sign of life about. The buildings were weathered but kept in good shape. They were plain and obviously built for use. He swung from the saddle beside the porch, and it was then, just as he was stepping onto the porch, that he saw the saddled horse that was tied round the corner.

"Anyone home?" he called loudly; and at once a scuff of boots came toward him from somewhere deep in the heart of the house. Tod Hackberry stood in the doorway and eyed him. "Come in," he invited; "I'll dig up a drink."

Hackberry's office was a plain, barren room without character. Neither shade nor drape softened the angles of its windows. The only furniture was a battered desk and a three-legged stool. The stool was occupied, held down by a sallow-cheeked, hatchet-faced man whose bright little eyes studied Connifay slyly.

Hackberry murmured, "Batista Wilkes. This's the gent that give Brady a mite more'n he could handle — goes by the name of Connifay, Wilkes. I —"

"Yes," Wilkes inserted, "I saw him tunnel your foreman, Tod." He watched them blandly, finding amusement in the sudden black stain of Hackberry's eyes.

Hackberry settled his shoulders against the wall by the door and got out a battered pipe and filled it. "There are some things, B'tiste, that are better forgot. Wilkes," he said to Connifay, "runs the Bug Wagon outfit, south an' east of Roblero Mountain."

"Yes," Connifay nodded, and looked at Wilkes. He was short, obese, and dressed in Levis that were patched and faded as the shirt above them. He had a pale and pointed face beneath the shabby, greenish-hued hat on his head. His eyes slid away from Connifay's but maintained their gleam of malicious guile. "I have met his kind in the gambling rooms."

Wilkes' sallow cheeks showed a touch of color. "You have seen them win, perhaps?"

Connifay said, "Quite often," and watched Hackberry get a bottle from his desk. He shook his head when Hackberry offered it. Wilkes took a long swig and smacked his lips. Hackberry put the bottle on the floor and leaned one hip against the desk's near corner.

"You figurin' to stay in this country awhile?"

"I've considered the idea."

Hackberry nodded, sucking smoke from his pipe. "Pressure is a argument. A man don't like to be shoved into anything."

"Ain't we all bein' shoved?" Wilkes' grin was sly as his eyes touched Connifay's. "Timpas' man Fargo, just got back from Mesilla. Happened to be down that way myself. Happened to be in the land office when Fargo come in. He recorded a quit-claim deed to Jackson's spread. In Timpas' name," he said, watching Hackberry.

The Currycomb boss put smoke around him. His voice, coming out of it, was coolly even. "Nothin' wrong with Jackson sellin' to Timpas."

"Kind of odd, though, Jackson dyin' right afterwards."

Wilkes' insinuating words brought a silence with them. The room held the pulse of unspoken thoughts. Connifay said: "What's Timpas after? Does anyone know?"

"Sure," Wilkes said. "I been tryin' to tell

these mutton-heads, but you can't get the fools to listen."

"He thinks — B'tiste, I mean, that Timpas is after this valley —"

"An' he is!" Wilkes exclaimed. "Wants the whole damn valley, lock, stock an' barrel!"

"It's not bad range, taken by an' large —"

"Not bad; but you've seen better an' so have I," Wilkes said. "He ain't after this range. Not for no cattle, I tell you —"

"The Wet Moon," Hackberry murmured, "is a syndicate, and syndicates bein' what they are —"

"Pah!" Wilkes snorted contemptuously. "There never was a fool like a cowman. Timpas may be a syndicate, but he cares no more about cattle than that!" He snapped *his* fingers with angry venom.

"You mean . . . sheep?" Connifay asked.

"He dunno what he means," growled Hackberry. "He's got Timpas on the brain. See Timpas' hand in every circumstance. Dreams of him prob'ly —"

"I'll tell you this," Wilkes said; "if we don't act quick he'll have us all out of here! Who do you think's behind all this night-ridin'? Behind the shootin' an' killin' goin' on in the hills? Behind the burnin's an' raidin's that's wreckin' this country?" He

150

picked up the bottle, thumped the desk top with it. "By grab, I say we'll either band together or we'll get run out of here!"

"By Timpas!" Hackberry sneered.

"By Timpas!"

"Which," asked Connifay, "is the biggest outfit round here, not counting Timpas'?"

"Kroniac's. Then Hackberry's Curry-comb; then my spread —"

Connifay said, "You reckon Timpas is workin' on Kroniac? Tryin', I mean, to smash the Fiddle-Back as a kind of lesson to the rest of you?"

But Wilkes apparently had talked all he aimed to. He was hoisting the bottle. When he set it down his mistrusting eyes were opaquely reflective. "Where do *you* come into this tintype?"

"I don't," smiled Connifay; and Wilkes smiled, too. He did not dispute the gambler's words.

He said to Hackberry: "When you figurin' to sell out, Tod?"

"Ain't given no thought to it," Hackberry answered.

A reflective silence settled then, Wilkes' cat eyes staring round inscrutably. "What's to prevent us three throwin' in together? Let Timpas hammer the Fiddle-Back down — there ain't much chance it'll take him long. When the smoke clears off us three can step in an' grab off the pot —"

"To what purpose?" Hackberry idly asked.

Wilkes shrugged fat shoulders. "If it's good for Mister Ely, it ought to be good for us."

Connifay gave them a dark appraisal. This Wilkes was a cunning, unscrupulous schemer, who used many words to cover his thinking. The Currycomb boss was of different caliber. He had the look of a strong-tempered man, yet the cool, tough slants of his weather-bronzed cheeks remained darkly taciturn and the black ends of a mustache drooped across his mouth to hide any edge of expression it loosed. An unsmiling man, gauntly dark and dangerous.

The fox and the wolf, Mark Connifay thought, and knew then what he had to do.

"Hear about Shain throwin' in with the Fiddle-Back?" he asked.

Wilkes' hatchet face changed grotesquely. His long jaw dropped. His eyes grew startled and swiftly angry. He had the look of a man unexpectedly slapped.

Hackberry said without visible expression: "I been lookin' for him to do that any day."

Wilkes swore and Hackberry's chin came

up. He leaned his bony shoulders forward and tapped the dottle out of his pipe. His questioning glance reached across to Connifay. Connifay's cheeks held smooth and Hackberry said:

"His aid won't change the shape of this much. Last week he was pullin' strong for Timpas. Changes his coat to every wind. Kroniac can have him an' welcome. That would be my thought come I was Ely."

Wilkes abruptly said to Connifay: "You ain't declared your intendin's yet. I'm a plain-talkin' man. I'd like to call your hand, friend. Let us see what you've got."

"Just a busted flush," Mark Connifay smiled. "As I said before, you can leave me out —"

"If you want to be out you ought to leave this country. It's in my mind you don't like Timpas no better than I do. Whether you do or not, Timpas don't like you. So the writin's plain. If Timpas can't plant you he will run you out."

"Mebbe he'll find me tired of runnin' —"

"Now," scowled Wilkes, "that's jest what I figgered! So why shouldn't you throw in with us? If you stay you'll have to fight 'im anyway. Singly we can't do a damn thing, but together —"

Hackberry said: "Hold on," and his

searching eyes probed Connifay darkly. "Mind tellin' me what yuh come out here for?"

"Thought I might hit you for a job."

"But yuh didn't."

"No."

Their eyes locked inscrutably. "Suppose," Hackberry said, "I was to offer yuh a job?"

"You'd probably regret it."

"Supposin' I was figurin' to bolster the Fiddle-Back — would that make any difference?"

"A man's got to live with himself, Tod."

"To hell with the riddles!" Hackberry said. "Come on; speak out! Y'u an' me could do things, by God. We got a lot in common, Connifay."

"Two pistols tucked in a belt."

"Ain't it so?" The Currycomb boss showed a narrow grin. "Would a pardnership deal interest yuh?"

Connifay caught the hard intentness of Wilkes' black stare. The man did not like this turn in the talk. Suspicion and anger were tightening his cheeks, and Connifay understood he had plans of his own.

Connifay's voice held an edge of regret. " 'Fraid not."

"Why?"

"Because there's a part of me, Tod, wouldn't get along with you."

"Riddles again! Why don't you say what you mean?" He gave the gambler's cheeks close scrutiny. "What is it?"

"Conscience, Tod."

"Yuh don't leave a man much pride!"

Connifay said regretfully: "Truth seldom does."

15. A Matter of Business

Ann Kroniac, driving the team with sparkling eyes and hair a-toss in the sunrise breeze, found the world bright-faced with promise. This was the road to Mesilla, and the invigorating tonic of the cool, crisp air made trouble seem a far-off thing, her doubts dispelled in the sunlight flooding this clean, fresh land. Even the rattle and bang of the jouncing wagon somehow seemed a merry, wholly satisfying tune.

She drove with a sure skill born of much practice, the loneliness of this wild country, the sunsplashed grandeur of these rimming mountains, lifting and exalting her, as the hills reassured her with their impregnable calm. There was peace in this land, in its quiet and beauty, in its far-flung vistas; for the first time in weeks Ann knew a feeling of security.

She thought of many things during the ride, but mostly she thought of the gambler, Connifay.

It was dusk when she reached Mesilla. She put up her team and, after an indifferent supper, went at once to her room and got into bed, not even the noise from the downstairs bar being able long to keep her awake.

After breakfast next morning she went round to the bank. Old Dan, the cashier, looked up with a smile; came forward to attend to her wants personally. "Howdy, Miz' Ann. You're looking pert. Warmin' up fer a scorcher — How's your Dad these days?"

"He'd be a lot easier in mind if you'd let us have a loan. This drought and —"

"There's nothing I'd like better than to tide you folks over. But these are bad times for cattle. We haven't made a ranch loan in three months — can't afford to. Why, only last week two El Paso banks closed their doors, crammed to the grills with stock-men's paper — vaults jammed with ranches they couldn't operate or even get rid of. I tell you —"

Ann's eyes were cold with an angry scorn, but she kept her indignant thoughts to herself. "How much is the Fiddle-Back good for?"

The old man shook his head sadly, shrugged and went back to consult a ledger. He pursed his lips, eyed the dark, beamed ceiling. "Ed," he called to the teller abruptly, "has the Fiddle-Back deposited anything lately — any sums you haven't listed?"

Young Ed, the teller, looked at Ann and nodded. To the cashier he said: "I don't guess they have, sir."

"You don't guess!" Ann said sharply. "Don't you *know?*"

"Yes, ma'am," the teller said, reddening, "they haven't." He made a discomfited pretense of being busy with the money stacked in piles on the counter.

Old Dan said: "Then your account stands now, Miz Ann, at three thousand, two hundred and ten dollars, exactly."

Ann said instantly: "There should be over eight thousand —"

"Perhaps you're forgetting the check Lesump cashed that day he was killed —"

"Check!" Ann stared at him, startled, suddenly bewildered and frightened. "What check? Tom never had any check —"

"But he did," Old Dan said quietly. "I cashed it for him myself, as it happens, and I remember the occasion distinctly. He came in just before noon and put through a check for five thousand. I've often wondered if perhaps it wasn't that money —"

"Do you mean to tell me Tom Lesump came in here and presented a check on the

Fiddle-Back for five thousand dollars, and you cashed it?"

"Certainly. Wasn't he in the habit of cashing Fiddle-Back checks?"

"Of course he was. But not for any such amount as that!"

Old Dan's pale gaze looked a little flinty. "All I know of the matter is that he presented the check and I cashed it. My understanding with your father —"

"I know all about that. Why wasn't Dad told of this sooner?"

"You ought to know how careless your father was in these matters. We've asked him time and again to bring his book in and — "

"But Tom Lesump was killed more than three months ago!"

"Three months and . . . seven days," said Old Dan, consulting the ledger. "Your father hasn't come in —"

He broke off, his spare frame suddenly rigid, a look of horror springing wide his incredulous stare.

Amazed at the man's queer actions, Ann turned to see what the cashier was looking at. Cold fear stopped the breath in her throat. Three masked men with leveled shotguns stood just inside the doors, grim and silent. The tall, cadaverous central figure wore crossed belts over his brush-clawed chaps, their holstered weapons slung butt forward. "Stick'em up!" he said, "An' you, too, lady!"

16. Killed in Mesilla

Ann swayed.

White and shaken with the shock of Old Dan's news, the sight of those presented weapons was almost enough to break her composure utterly. But something of her father's stubborn nature was in her blood and she would not faint; she would not let herself. She obeyed, as did Old Dan and the teller, and raised her hands, though her heart was pounding. But she could not drag her gaze from the robbers.

They were booted and spurred, dressed in workaday garb. Had their scarfs been left down about their necks they might well have been taken for honest riders. But they weren't — they were outlaws, without faith or principle, without scruple or mercy. They were here on business and they meant to effect it. Already the tall man, and one of the others, had gone behind the grilled partition; the tall man's grating tones were ordering Ed and Old Dan to open the doors of the man-high safe. Young Ed's voice raised in vociferous pro-

161

test. An impatient curse ripped out of the tall man. A gun shot filled the place with clamor. Ann saw the teller go reeling back with his jaws stretched wide in a cry unheard through the racketing echoes. From the street outside, split seconds later, came the swift *crack! crack!* of a high-powered rifle; she heard one man's lifted voice say clearly: "Git back, you fools, or I'll let you hev it!"

Now a heavy silence clutched the bank, a quiet quick-woven from the stuff of nightmares. Ann gazed toward the rear, toward the bank's big safe. She saw that its doors were standing wide. Saw the shorter outlaw nervously holding a sack which the cadaverous leader was rapidly filling with bags of coins and bundled currency.

She yearned to flee but dared not move. The man by the doorway was derisively watching her above the obscuring folds of his neckerchief.

It was hard to believe she was sharing a part in this — bitter to feel she was so impotent. More bitter by far was the lifting scorn she felt for cowardly men of this town who could stand back and watch without lifting a finger. It was plain these raiders had them buffaloed. There must be three or four outlaws on guard outside.

She could hear them laugh, calling taunts to the townsmen. And suddenly Ann was furiously angry. These robbers were killing Fiddle-Back's last slim chance for survival.

She saw the man in the doorway abruptly stiffen — caught the flutter of hoofs — quick oaths — a high, shrill whistle. The cadaverous tall man and his squat companion hurried into the lobby, dragging their sack.

Out yonder a rifle cracked, two more reports lifting into it instantly. Ann saw the masked man in the entrance spin, cursing. With an excited yell he abandoned the others and dashed outside. The tall and the squat man let go of their sack and came lunging forward, clawed hands driving hipward.

Through the heightened clamor of discharged rifles Ann could hear the hoofs of the oncoming horseman. They were lacing the din like a call, like a challenge; and abruptly the firing redoubled in volume, sound buffeting the buildings in ragged blasts as the townsmen rallied and began throwing in lead with mounting enthusiasm.

Dust rose thickly, swirling into the lobby, as the men outside flung into their saddles. The cadaverous man slammed his words at them wickedly. "Wait! Wait, you sons!"

He jumped to the bank's still-open doors, cursing horribly as he emptied his pistol at the fleeing horsemen. "They've taken our broncs, the —"

He flung himself desperately clear of the doorway as the squat man beside him jackknifed, screeching with both convulsed hands clapped over his belly.

The cadaverous leader, trapped and frantic, ran past Ann, thumbing cartridges into his emptied six-shooter. Before she could move a man's black shape blotted light from the entrance. She saw flame streak from the gun in his hand.

She could hear the shots striking; saw the tall man lurch, saw the red blood dribbling through the clutch of his fingers, saw the awful fear that was twisting his face. His scarf had dropped loose and he stood revealed for the darkfaced Fargo — Timpas' Wet Moon range boss.

He was crouched, at bay, trying to bring up the pistol that he still had hold of. He put both hands to the task, but the barrel of the weapon drooped lower and lower; he could not summon the power to raise it.

Ann closed her eyes but she heard him strangle; heard his final gasp as he collapsed on the floor.

Ann knew without looking when the man left the doorway; knew he had gone without coming inside. And though her only view had been brief, silhouetted, she knew who it was. No other man would have gone away and left that money where Fargo had dropped it.

The sun beat down with a heightened fury as Ann pushed through the crowd about the doorway. The morbid and curious had gathered like buzzards now that danger no longer restrained them. It was indecent, she thought, the way they stood and stared, pointing out this and that to each other, commenting on all the gory details, calling up things they had seen in times past. Ann held her skirts close and hurried past them with her glance determinedly held straight ahead. She wanted to get away from this scene and this town, but there was something she had to do first. She saw a knot of more substantial-looking citizens standing before a saloon several doors away.

The men looked up at her approach. Two or three thought to remove their hats. "Things all right at the bank, Miss? That stranger allowed they was an' said —"

"You saw him then? Which way did he

go?" Ann asked, a little breathlessly.

They looked at her curiously. "Why, that there's his horse right back of you, ma'am. I — I think he went in there," one of the older men said, a jerk of his thumb indicating the saloon.

"Would you tell him I'd like to speak with him, please?"

One of the younger men spoke up brusquely. "I reckon not. We done quit fetchin' an' packin' fer the Fiddle-Back, ma'am. Yore father ain't cock o' this roost no more an' —"

"Meaning, I suppose," Ann said resentfully, "that someone else is. Mister Timpas, perhaps?"

"That's correct. Mister Timpas, ma'am."

"And so you'll bow and scrape for Mister Timpas now. Even though," Ann told them scornfully, "it was Timpas' range boss, Fargo, who was doing his best to rob your bank."

The man said without change of expression: "If Fargo was bossin' them roughs, he was bossin' 'em. But that don't prove Mister Timpas —"

Ann's pride rebelled against talking with such men. She lifted her chin and moved away from them. It made no difference to such as they who managed the country's destiny, just so they were leagued on that man's side. Coyotes, she thought contemptuously, who would run for the brush at the drop of a hat.

Ann's pride rebelled against talking with such men. She subsequently did. Perhaps she hoped to shame them; hoped to find that one among them might discover the courtesy to do what it seemed she intended doing for herself. But no one did.

Ann found herself at the doors of the saloon. She could feel the stares of the men behind her; but pride would not let her back down now. She pushed through the batwings. Several men grouped along the bar regarded her askance. Most of them dragged off their hats but none looked with favor upon her intrusion. Their glances said plainly she'd no business there.

Ann said tightly: "I was told I'd find Mark Connifay in here. Will someone of you kindly call him for me?"

One after another they turned their backs and took up their talk where her entrance had silenced it.

Cheeks white with anger, Ann saw Mark Connifay coming toward her from a maze of tables at the rear of the place. He stopped a few feet from her and, removing his hat, regarded her inscrutably. "Were you —"

"I was," Ann told him huskily and, turning with a twirl of skirts, almost fled through the barroom's batwings.

Connifay, through the sun's bright warmth, tramped after her without speaking, his lean cheeks darkly taciturn, his pace showing neither haste nor reluctance. Whatever his thoughts he did not disclose them. From storefronts and hitchrails men turned to regard them but, like Ann's, Connifay's glance refused them existence. His boots drew hollow bursts of sound from the places where the walk was planked; the rowels of his spurs made a tinkling chorus across the quiet of the gone-still street.

Ann's look was bitter when she stopped by the open gate of the livery. She was furiously aware that she had had no business going into that barroom; and with the awareness had come realization of how irretrievably that brashness had linked her name with Mark Connifay's. In the clutch of her turbulent feelings she believed the gambler had known she would follow him — had gone into that place deliberately that he might complete her humiliation, and her resentment was fed additional fuel when he said with just the trace of a smile: "If you felt yourself compelled to thank me —"

"To thank you!" she blazed, and looked at him bitterly, her lifted chin trembling under the lash of her anger. "To think you've got the cheek to stand there and throw my brother's debts in my face!"

"Brother's debts?" He stared. Comprehension suddenly gleamed in his eyes. "If you mean them notes, I'd already forgotten them. I've been amply repaid by the discomfort their loss has caused Mister —" He broke off with a shrug. Smiling queerly, he said: "No thanks are due —"

"Are you trying to imply" — Ann looked curiously startled — "that you got those notes from — from somebody else?"

Connifay said drily: "I'm not in the habit of playing cards with boys."

She did not resent the words — did not hear them. All her cherished conceptions were up in arms, disturbed, chaotic; and there was a song in her heart that pride could not stifle, and she was amazed to find all her anger dissolved, banished in the humbling knowledge that once again she had misjudged this man.

She stared down at her hands, saying nothing, thinking back in her mind to their other encounters. Connifay was not of the breed that show their feelings; she had always sensed this. But now she recalled little things that had got past his guard — things, had she realized, that must have revealed the real personality hidden behind his gambler's mask. Considering these, she found it hard to think of him as a card-sharping tinhorn, a man quick to gunplay and violent reprisal.

She remembered her uncle's words and nodded, seeing things closer to their true perspective. In a sudden, impulsive surge of contrition she wished she might ask Connifay's pardon for the things she had done — for the unfair things said to him. But her pride rebelled at such self-abasement. She could never go to him. He must come to her.

And the moment was lost. She looked up to find him staring down-street, at the disintegrating crowd moving away from the bank in little, excitedly talking knots.

Seeming to feel her gaze, he looked around, and there was a subtle mockery in the faint trace of smile he showed her; and with heat in her cheeks she demanded sharply: "Did you deliberately follow me to Mesilla?"

"No. Fargo followed you. I followed

Fargo. Fortunate, wasn't it?"

"In what way?" she said coldly.

"Where would your Fiddle-Back be if Fargo had gotten away with that robbery?"

In sudden despair she said: "Can it matter?" and told him of the unexpected check which Old Dan claimed Tom Lesump had cashed — Tom Lesump, their former range boss, who was now beyond all questioning.

"You say he was killed?" Connifay was eyeing her oddly.

"Yes," she said in a hopeless way that closed Mark Connifay's teeth like a vise. "Killed the same day the check was cashed. Why — why," she cried, noticing his look, "you don't think — you — you don't think the check was a forgery, do you?"

"Such things have been known to happen."

She looked at him, startled, her mind upset by conjecture again. It seemed incredible, and yet — it was possible. Knowing her father's carelessness in such matters it would be an easy thing for someone at the bank to . . . Tom Lesump had been a man of ingrained loyalty, a veteran cowman and staunch adherent to Fiddle-Back interests. He'd been her father's right hand for more years than she could remember. A personal and outspoken friend of old Andre's . . . a man who had seen eye to eye with him.

"Here — wait!" she cried. "Where are you going?"

His turned head revealed a remote kind of smile. "I think I'll go have a talk with that banker."

The cashier's stare showed frightened eyes. He backed off a little and appeared to shrink. He fingered his collar nervously. "What — what did you want?"

Connifay said: "We've come back for a talk. You better take us into your office. You won't want the town listenin' in on this."

The old man eyed them for a long, still moment. Seeming older than ever, he led the way through the grill and down a dark passageway, finally showing them into a small shabby office. Connifay came at once to the point. "Miz' Ann has come to close the Fiddle-Back account. My name is Connifay. I'm here to see she gets a square deal. You will pay her, in cash, eight thousand, two hundred an' ten dollars. Now."

The cashier started to say something. But whatever it was, it died on the way. A nerve jerked along one side of his face and the hand he put out to brace himself trembled.

He got them the money, afterwards sinking into the chair by his desk like a man gone blind. He was still there, blankeyed and motionless, when they left his office.

"I — I'm not sure I understand you."

Outside, Ann turned to Connifay. "I don't —"

"Don't try. No thanks are necessary." His lifted glance went to the Organ ramparts. "It's gettin' late," he said. "You've a long drive ahead of you. Better grab a bite an' get started."

"You're not going back with me?"

"Back? You mean to Single Cinch?"

Their eyes met and locked. "To the ranch," Ann said; but he shook his head.

"Not tonight —"

"Then," she said, enlivened by the hope she found in his words, "you'll be out when you can — tomorrow possibly?"

She watched him closely, but his gambler's cheeks gave no hint of his thoughts and she wisely kept silent as they walked up the road toward the livery. In his own time and way he would answer.

But Connifay's answer when it finally

came was far from being of the sort she had looked for; it came as a question. "How long do you reckon you could get along with me?"

"All right," he said, "let's put it this way. The Fiddle-Back is up against something — something big and bad, by the looks of it. Somebody's out to smash it; somebody that wants it, lock, stock an' barrel, and if I was going to bet I'd say they'll get it . . . the way things stand right now anyway. Now you've made it plain you've no use for me personally. I'm a card-sharping tinhorn, a cheat and a killer — a 'mad dog.' Remember?"

The smile went off his mouth abruptly. "A man don't change like that, Miz' Ann. There ain't no lamp you can rub that will change him. You can't make a silk purse out of a sow's ear — nor a sow's ear out of a silk purse, neither. I'm still the gambler you hated yesterday. I'm still Mark Connifay, the 'mad dog' killer. Are you aimin' to stomach these things for the sake of hirin' my speed with a pistol?"

She fell back before the scorn in his eyes. The bitter things he had said seemed true, and she caught one hand to her throat, cheeks crimson. But she did not blame him. She wanted to tell him how wrong he was — that it wasn't his speed with a gun that she sought — that his judgment was as harshly unjust as her own, of him, had so recently been. But how could she tell him of the things in her heart — the things she would say but could find no words for? She heard him laugh coldly and tears stung her eyes as she caught his shape wheeling. "Mark —" She reached blindly.

Her hand brushed his sleeve and he stopped, arrested. He did not turn to look at her, though. The half-rolled smoke became shreds in his fingers. "All right," he said in a ragged rush of breath. "Get your rig an' I'll ride with you. But I make no promises — remember it."

It was almost midnight when Connifay drove Ann's team into the hock-deep dust of Single Cinch. He slowed the wagon where dapples of light from the noisy saloon crisscrossed the humped shapes of a line of racked horses.

With a murmured oath he stopped the team; so short the jerked ponies came back on their haunches. With a brusque, "Back directly," he thrust the lines into Ann's hands and was gone in the shadows.

All the miles from Mesilla, which they'd covered in silence, he'd been telling him-

self what a fool he would be to let sentiment throw him with the Fiddle-Back. But
he'd known all the time he was going to —
was quite sure he understood why he was,
too. He was going to because of Ann
Kroniac; because she had roused something in him that was stronger than himself.

There were times, he decided, when
being a fool could have a lot of compensa-
tions. Perhaps it was consideration of these
which put a second's hard smile on his lips
as he opened the saloon's back door and
stepped in.

There was color and confusion in the
place tonight. Evidently some outfit had
paid off its hands. Fiddle squeals and
banjo strummings vied with the thumps of
boot and voices talking as gyrating couples
whirled and whooped and round-the-wall
watchers bellowed crass comments.

Connifay lounged by the door. He remained unremarked for a good dozen moments; then the barkeep saw him and
moved forward, casually stopped beside
Shain and Wilkes.

He waited till the fiddlers stopped. In
that comparative lull he said quite clearly:
"Spendin' your split of the bank loot,
boys?"

17. "You Damn' Card Sharper!"

You could feel the brittle quiet closing down.

Vidal Shain went rigid against the bar and his yellow eyes became tight cracks with no expression in them. But the fat man, Wilkes, was slower. His owlish look appeared to be turning it over. You could see the impact of it finally hit him. His face wrinkled up and he cursed the gambler with shaking lips.

Mark Connifay smiled. There was a quizzical humor in the slant of his eyes, a certain grim enjoyment in his consideration of the pair. "You ought to be more careful about the horseflesh you ride if you don't want folks knowin' what you been up to." His smile flashed wide and suddenly reckless. "Last look I had at you boys you was fannin' it to hell an' gone away from the Mesilla Bank."

With a scream of rage Wilkes threw his glass full into Connifay's face. "That's a damn' lie!" he shrilled. "Why you —"

Connifay's fist jammed the rest in his throat. All across the room men surged to their feet and those by the bar made a dash to get elsewhere. Wilkes was tugging desperately at a hung-up gun and somebody — a slat-built fellow in bullhide chaps — made a flying dive and caught Connifay's arm in a grip like a vise.

A tight crack of smile creased Connifay's lips. He ignored the man's hold; slid his free left fist inside his shirt and brought it out with a short-barreled gun that clicked to full cock as it centered on Wilkes.

Wilkes' hand left his weapon in jittery haste.

Derision looked out of Connifay's glance. "You're a mite too fat to be playin' with a pistol. Call off your dog before I bore you, Wilkes."

The slat-built fellow let go of his arm, and with a sullen scowl backed off beside Wilkes.

"Only curs," Mark said, "would leave a pardner trapped like you skunks left Fargo. We ought to ride you out of this place on a rail. If there was a few honest men here I 'low we would; but the rest of this crew ain't much taller than snakes — I said 'snakes' case some of you gents didn't hear."

You could see they heard, but nobody spoke.

Connifay's laugh had a scraped-tin sound. He raked Shain and Wilkes with a scathing glance. "Get into your saddles an' hit the breeze. Don't come back or they'll bury you here."

He looked at the crowd then, seeming to memorize each face. His stare, cold and saturnine, stopped on Joe Brady by the end of the bar. "Mebbe you better pull *your* freight, too. The next gent I catch messin' round with the Fiddle-Back is goin' to get started for hell in a hurry."

There'd be no doubt now where he stood, he guessed. The range would be buzzing like mad before morning. He had laid down his challenge and Timpas would know of it before noon the next day.

He ought, he supposed, to feel somber and worried. He didn't, though. He felt considerably better than he'd felt in days. The prospect of danger — of Timpas' wild anger when he got the report of these things Mark had said — appeared strangely stimulating to a man whose intention had been to avoid trouble.

He was smilingly quartering toward the street when a hand came out of the blackness and stopped him. Bella Mae's voice said: "You fool! Are you *loco?*"

She was just a vague blur against the

dark planking. "Don't you know these hills are salted with fellows hunting with guns for the price on your head?"

"What do you reckon I should do?" he smiled.

"Do! Get out of here! Get out quick — I told you that the first night I saw you! Fancy talk won't bluff this crowd; they mean business. Ely Timpas means to have this valley if he has to kill every damfool in it! And he's already started!" Bella Mae dropped her voice. "Three small spreads were raided last night, their buildings wrecked, their cattle slaughtered. Timpas is filin' —"

"I thought," Mark said, "you was a friend of Ely's. Why tip me —"

"There's a lot of difference between tellin' an' provin'. I don't like to see you used by them Kroniacs. I'm tryin' to drive some sense in your head so you'll get to hell out of here before you get planted! Don't be a lunkhead! You can't stop Timpas — you can't even hurt him. The *law* can't hurt him — he's bought the sheriff out body an' soul. I tell you, this thing's all set. All you'll do is get yourself killed."

"I might," Mark said, "take some others —"

"D'you think it matters to Timpas how many you kill? All he cares about is getting this valley, and you've gone an' played right into his hands. The death of every man killed will be blamed on *you!* My God, Mark! Don't laugh. Can't you *see?*"

"I can see you're hysterical."

She said in a sudden rush of breath: "Look! You got a bad name in this country — you got a bad name in Texas. Ely knows — he took the trouble to find out about you — about the men you shot at Smith's Crossing — about that nester you killed north of Lubbock. And Bannock! Plenty guys saw you kill Bannock, and they'll say whatever they're told to say — Ely will see to that. Do you know what he calls you? — 'that gun-crazy card-sharp'! He's got a lot of weight up to Santa Fe and he'll use every bit of it to see that you're blamed for this. *You'll* be the one who's started this — you, and Kroniac who'll be payin' your wages! And you'll be the one to get swung —"

"So he's already got me swung, has he!"

"Mark!" She caught at his arm, and his attempt to free it only pulled her closer. He abruptly wondered if this talk weren't a trap — weren't some new trick of Timpas' devising. Then the thought went away. The

181

girl was too tense, too obviously earnest to be acting.

He forgot about Ann, that she was waiting. Bella Mae said on an indrawn breath: "What's it to you if these galoots kill each other? What do you care? You're a fool to get into it — ain't I warned you plenty?" She said, her voice changing: "Is it because of that girl? Old Kroniac's daughter? Is it *her* you're —"

"I reckon you've ridden that trail far enough."

In that moment of silence he could feel the heat of her glare through the dark. She said with sudden contempt: "Well — I've warned you. If you want to bat your head against the Kroniac pride an' get your damn life beat out for the trouble —"

She let his arm go; flung away from him angrily. "What do you want with her? Think she's worth bein' killed for? What could she give you — respectability?" Her laugh was brittle. "That's pretty cold comfort for a man that wants something warm in his bed. Mark — get your eyes open! Why gawp for the moon when you got somethin' a sight more useful right under your hand?"

When it became evident he wasn't going to answer, she said in a tone of withering scorn: "Do you suppose the little fool would marry a gambler with her old man hatin' the breed worse than poison? Them kids've been raised with the idea they're second cousins to *God!* He'd sooner see the *devil* get that blond-headed baggage than see her tied up with a gamblin' man!

"Do you reckon she'd ever hitch up with a killer? — That's what they'll call you before this gets done with! She'd despise you for the very talent that's makin' them want to hire you now! I know that old man — how I know him! Harder than gun steel an' prouder than sheep dip! His father was a colonel of Confederate cavalry who ruined himself at a Yankee's card table. What could a girl sprung out of such stock —"

She broke off to grab Connifay's arm again fiercely. "You shan't go like this — you've *got* to listen! You can't help them anyway. Get out of this, Mark, an' take me with you. You can't stop Timpas. Believe me! Nothing will ever stop him but —"

She jammed the back of a hand to her mouth. Her shape went tense against the wall's blackness.

But the thought was out. "But death, eh?" Mark said.

"You can't, Mark — you can't!" Her voice was breathless as she crowded against him. "I was crazy to say a fool thing like that! He'd kill you quick as he killed Whoa Jackson — you wouldn't have a chance! He wouldn't fight fair. He'd wait —"

"Like Bannock?"

"Oh — can't you see? Can't you *see?*"

The hand on his arm closed tighter and tighter and her voice, gone husky, was almost a wail. "Mark! What — what have I *done?*"

Her face came around and he caught the wet gleam of tears on her lashes and, suddenly, she was fully against him, hands clutching his shirt, face buried against it, the soft curls of her hair gently brushing his chin. The ache of her hunger was a knife in his heart, but he could not give her the answer she wanted; could not —

Of a sudden she felt him go stiff, head up, listening.

In that moment each became aware of the receding sound of a wagon.

Contrite with remembrance of Ann waiting for him, Connifay broke the girl's hold, was swiftly making his departure when she caught him again. Hoarse with emotion, her breathing was ragged. "You can't!" she cried fiercely. "You can't quit me this way! You can't stop Timpas and you'll never have his girl — yes, *his* girl! You fool! Didn't you *know?* He proposed to her twice — *he's mad for her* — and both times she turned him down; and now he swears he'll have his will of her if he has to kill her getting it! Now do you see —"

But Connifay was gone, plunging through the night's blackness toward the road, seeing — *yes!* seeing all too well how the Brady hell-cat had tricked him, holding him there while —

He came into the empty road and froze. His horse was there, standing on dropped reins, but Ann and the wagon were nowhere in sight. He peered through the windwhipped dark without luck. There was no sign of the team. He could not hear the wagon for the rough-house racket coming out of the saloon. He swore — was still swearing when he went through the batwings with a gun in each fist.

Talk and music jarred into silence.

In that startled hush every head was turned toward the man who stood so stiffly by the doorway, stood so bitterly eyeing them above cocked guns.

"Where is she?"

His words got no answer. Neither Wilkes nor Shain was among the crowd facing him. A number of men shifted weight uneasily. The moments began to crawl and get edgy. The burning glitter of Connifay's state was like a curse put on them, rooting them with its threat of violence. The nearest man, bony-shouldered and gaunt above his bullhide chaps, rasped a cottony tongue across dry lips. A man behind him abruptly spat derisively.

The spitter was the Fiddle-Back foreman, Grote.

Connifay spoke to the other man. "Thought I advised you to start makin' tracks?"

The gaunt man shivered. A kind of a tremor got into his legs. He had to prime his lips before he could speak, and then his words were so thick as to be hardly intelligible. "Was goin' —"

"Then what are you waitin' for?"

The man brushed past him, breathing raggedly. Connifay said: "Where is she, Grote?"

Grote sneered. "If you're meanin' Miz' Ann, she's done gone home."

Connifay said consideringly: "Home, eh? How do you know?"

"Hell, I talked with her, didn't I?"

"What did she say?"

Grote grinned hugely. "Said if I saw you to tell you she expected the Fiddle-Back

186

could rock along without no help from alley-mashin' card sharps —"

Connifay struck him across the mouth.

Grote's red face bloated poisonously. One down-shoved hand spread above his holster, but he dared not draw with that gun in Connifay's left hand covering him. He said, hoarse with rage: "Put up that cutter an' by Gawd I'll kill you!"

"I'm a little too busy to be killed tonight. How much does the time sheet owe you?"

That talk caught Grote off balance, confusing him, wrinkling his congested features. He was still that way, still probing the Texan's meaning, when Connifay took some gold coins from a pocket and tossed them down at Grote's booted feet.

An ugly suspicion deepened back of Grote's stare.

Connifay said: "I expect that'll cover anything you got comin'. You're all through at the Fiddle-Back — savvy? You can rattle your hocks any time you've a mind to."

The words took a moment to sink into Grote's brain. Fury came into his blazing eyes. Temper clawed caution clean out of him. With a strangled oath he got hold of his pistol. Gun thunder shook the lamps of the place and the glint of the range boss' pistol went skittering across six feet of floor. Grote crouched with his eyes like saucers, incredulously staring at his empty hand.

He was still crouched, staring, with his cheeks gone ashen, when Connifay's spurs quit the walk outside.

With the flat of his palm he had branded Grote's words a lie — but deep inside him Mark Connifay believed the man. Not the man's words, but the fact behind them. It appeared to Connifay entirely likely that Ann had either seen or heard some portion of that alley episode so neatly staged by smart Bella Mae. It may, partly, have been done for her benefit instead, as he'd first guessed, of having been brewed up to keep him busy while Ann, under one excuse or another, was lured away by Wilkes or Shain or some other of the hired guns in Timpas' pay. Ann, incensed by what she must have felt was a gross violation of right and decency or, at best, a lovers' quarrel with which she could have no concern, had whipped up her team and gone angrily home.

He could not blame her. This widening of the breach in their never comfortable relations was but another manifestation of the ironic hand at the helm of destiny. All his yesterdays had been built of such mischances. That nester north of Lubbock, for instance. The man had once been a hand of Mark's father's, a staunch supporter in that water-rights feud. On a certain day, long after the feud's last shot had been fired, Mark had gotten a note from the man. He had needed some money to swing some kind of a deal for cattle, the note said, and Mark, who'd been banking faro at the Orient House in Pecos, had closed his game and set off at once to see what he could do for the nester. The note had been handed him by a stranger, some bullwhacker passing through on his way to Fort Davis. There'd been nothing to rouse Mark's suspicions in that; emigrants' courtesy was the fastest way to get your wants across two hundred miles of prairie in unsettled times such as these were. He'd set out at once and got to Lubbock and the nester's holdings but a matter of minutes after the man had been dropped by a pistol fired sufficiently close to have left its powder marks on him — but a matter of minutes, yet in ample time to be discovered by Silver Dollar with his hand — Mark's hand — on the killer's left-behind pistol.

Connifay thought about this, and other things, as he rode morosely through the chill dark of early morning, bound once more for the Fiddle-Back. They would probably make no bones about telling him he was not wanted, he thought; that was one of those chances a man had to take when his trail was tangled as Connifay's was. But this was the way he had found life always; travail and turmoil, suspicion and hatred, a fleeting smile — perhaps the clasp of a friendly hand once or twice and finally, inevitably, oblivion. He would like to believe that life could be different, but he had never found it so.

There was a deep and gnawing sadness in him as he breathed of the wind flowing off the Organs, strong with the smell of wet timber and grasses. He was caught in the jaws of destiny again and his mind plucked forlornly at the edges of hungers felt but indefinable. And then, as the gray of false dawn crept across the crags, the Fiddle-Back ranch yard unfolded before him, constricting his muscles with the sight of raised rifles.

Four mounted men sat broncs by the gate post, each with his gun grimly focused on Connifay. It was like something seen below the Border, a firing squad at the break of day. There was no hint of friendliness on those bleak faces — nothing save bitter and hard-held anger.

It was then Mark saw the horse by the bunkhouse. The lathered bay with its head downswung between braced legs that were foam-flecked and quivering.

Grote's horse!

Connifay's throat went dry as dust. There was no sign of Ann or the team or the wagon.

Silver Dollar's hands, where they gripped his rifle, were the cold hard color of Yukon ice.

"You damn' card-sharper!" Tony cried. "Where is she?"

On the heels of his words flame streaked from the bunk house.

18. The Wet Moon Outfit

The flat, dry crack of a rifle spread its thinning echoes against the hills. Long before they had quieted Mark Connifay reeled, arms wide, from the saddle.

He lay without movement, grotesquely crumpled with his face in the dirt and one arm doubled under him.

Thirty seconds of silence were abruptly broken by the rasp of a door and the sound of approaching boots. Silver Dollar's thin lips pulled back in a sneer. "D'you always get your turkey cold, Grote?" And the cook, in a high shaken voice, said: "There's a name for a man that'll shoot from cover."

Kroniac said, harsh with anger: "Of all the sorry things you've done —"

"By heaven," shouted Grote, "a fella'd think I'd done this spread a mortal hurt, killin' that stinkin' card-sharpin' girl snatcher! If you don't like my style —"

"Be still. Have you figured out how we're to find where Ann is, now that you've pot-shot the man you claim hid her?"

Grote scowled, startled. "Hell! I done forgot —"

"An' here's somethin' else you 'done forgot.' "

That was Connifay's cool, soft drawl, and Connifay's eyes were maliciously glinting behind the cocked stare of a .44 pistol.

For a second Grote's look was ludicrous. Then all his features seemed to run together and flame leaped twice from his hip before, with a gasping, lurching stagger, his backbone buckled and dropped him slanchways.

With his eyes coldly watchful, Connifay rose. He sheathed his still-smoking pistol and stood slack with his back to the rump of his horse. Both of Grote's shots, like his try from the bunkhouse, appeared to have gone completely wild. "That's what comes," Mark said, "of bein' too eager. You might remember that, Silver, case you got notions."

Silver Dollar sneered, but Kroniac got down from his saddle and plowed through the dust to kneel beside Grote.

"You'll get nothin' out of him," Mark said, and the prediction proved well founded. Grote was dying and knew it, but he wasn't talking. All the old man's questions got but one reply. "Go ask that damn gambler!" That was all he would say.

Connifay rolled up a smoke and watched them dourly. When Grote's head fell back and Kroniac rose, with his glance like flint and his jaw muscles corded, Connifay said: "I'm goin' after Ann. How about a fresh horse?"

"You don't need no horse in the place where you're goin'!"

That was Silver, with his thumb whitely hauling back the hammer of his rifle.

Old Andre's eyes hit the man like a mallet. "Have you more regard for your feud with this man than you have for your niece's safety?"

Silver's roan face showed a flushed resentment. "You've got no call to talk that way. You heard what Grote said about this fellow —"

"Have you heard what 'this fellow' has to say about Grote?"

"At least I've got wit enough not to put any stock in it!"

Old Andre judged him and turned his back. He said to Connifay bluntly: "Do you know where my daughter is?"

"I think I can find her."

Kroniac's eyes bored through him sharply, trying to read some expression in that tough, locked face. He said: "There are things in you, Connifay, I never would have looked to find in a gambler. I asked you once to take a job with the Fiddle-Back. You didn't want it. Do you want it now?"

"What about Ann?"

"I'm thinking about Ann. But somebody's got to hold down this ranch or that thieving Timpas will lug off the door bolts. If I give you a horse can I —"

"Just give me the horse!"

The old man pointed to his own saddled Morgan.

It was ten miles to town, but Connifay, before covering a quarter of the distance, swung the horse off the trail at a westerly angle. He was remembering Bella Mae's words about Timpas; was remembering, too, that Wilkes and Shain had not been there when he'd gone back into the saloon and seen Grote. At the time he had thought nothing of it, had naturally supposed the pair had taken his advice and were on their way out of the country.

But now another thought took hold of him. It had plainly been in Kroniac's mind that Ann had been kidnapped with the idea of pulling the Fiddle-Back's remaining forces away from the ranch in a search for her. This notion coincided with one of Mark's own. Ann had had better than eight thousand dollars on her, and if the bank had been able to get word to him Timpas may have staged this deal for a double purpose that would well be worth all the risk he was taking. But careful thought made it seem more likely that the girl had been grabbed by Shain and Wilkes, in which case the range of possible motives was widened. Revenge against Connifay may have moved them to do it. There was hate to consider, the pair's hatred for Kroniac. There was also, and this was what Connifay now was scared of, Timpas' passion for the girl herself. Any way you looked at it, Wet Moon seemed bound to be the girl's destination.

Mark tried to figure how he would have handled this thing had he been in the boots of Vidal Shain — for he was sure it was Shain who'd be bossing the job. In Shain's boots he'd want to be rid of the girl as swiftly as might be, for the way of this region with kidnappers, with girl stealers, was apt to be short and quite permanent. Only the country's upset condition could have emboldened the pair into being so brash, and once embarked on the venture they would not be like to dally much till they'd gotten the girl off their hands.

Mark took the shortest way that he knew, and breakfast could hardly have been much more than over before he sighted the buildings of Timpas' headquarters. It was a big place, all the structures built of double adobes, with a long sprawling ranch house, flat-topped and parapeted, set square in the center of its shadeless yard. With that flat stretch of baked adobe around it, unbroken by even a blade of grass, the place looked more like a fort or a prison than it did the headquarters of a working cow ranch.

Connifay's mind absorbed detail with the subconscious ease of habit. There was a story in the mass of those buildings, in the downpulled slant of the Stet hat that was shading the face of a pole-sitter yonder — in the emptiness of the yard itself. These stories Connifay understood; they were geared to a pattern of violence, and that was something Mark knew by heart.

He stopped the lope of his horse by the gate, came through it and didn't bother closing it afterwards. Still in the saddle, he came up to the sitter and watched the man read the animal's brand. When the man's eyes lifted Connifay said: "Timpas around this morning?"

The man on the top rail shrugged. "Ain't seen him." He spread out his arms along the peeled pole, closed his hands round its weathered wood firmly. A tall fellow stepped from the bunkhouse. The man on the rail called without stirring: "Ain't seen Timpas around, hev you, Wally?"

The tall man came up on Connifay's left, stopped to scratch his back on a corral post. "Not real lately — why? This gent wantin' to see him?" His regard of the visitor was casually indifferent, and Connifay smiled a little, thinly.

He had known this man in Texas. He was a cheap gun-notching warrior who had adopted the sobriquet of "Willow Creek" to set him apart from other Wallies.

Connifay eyed them taciturnly and hoisted his shoulders and slid out of the saddle. "I'll just take a look," he said quietly.

"Sure. Go ahead," the rail sitter said. "How are things goin' in the card-sharpin' business?"

"I get along," Mark answered. "How are you gun renters makin' it?" He saw a deep red creep up Willow Creek's neck, but the man knew better than to make something of it. Connifay's lips curled contemptuously. "I'm leavin' this horse right here, Willow Creek, and it better be here when I come back for it."

There was a sulky brilliance in the gunfighter's eyes, but he wheeled without words and went off toward the saddle shed. Connifay looked at the yellow-haired man. "Mebbe you better come with me, Buff."

The rail sitter shrugged and climbed down from his perch.

"I guess," Mark said, "we'll try the house first."

"You're goin' to a mighty pile of work for nothin'."

"Your time's paid for. Get movin'."

There were horses in the corral and, as the man led off toward the house, Mark took another look at them, but without seeing any he could recognize. They would hardly have left her horse around, though; and while he was pretty well convinced by the men's acquiescence that Ann, if she'd been there, was there no longer, he wasn't passing up any bets in the matter. It would be better to look than to wish he had later.

But the house was empty.

"I expect you're doin' pretty good with this outfit. Timpas offered me a hundred an' twenty a month, with bonuses. Even an ordinary hand like you," Mark said, watching him, "ought to be saltin' away plenty when you consider the risk tied up with a girl snatchin'."

"Girl snatchin'!" The man's jaw dropped and his cheeks lost color.

Connifay said: "Didn't they tell you? Ann Kroniac with a team an' wagon completely vanished north of town last night."

He let the man think about that awhile, then said:

"C'mon. We'll try the bunkhouse now. After that we'll look in the root cellar and any other little hideouts you might have around this outfit. C'mon, snake — wriggle."

The man's glance was sullen. Anger twitched at his pulled-back lips, but Connifay's eyes were clouded agate. The man had been in the Cap and Ball the night Cash Bannock went over the railing. Memory of that moved him now. Connifay's growled "Mosey!" set him off with a smothered curse.

They moved again through the silent house, boot heels setting up a hollow clamor, metallic-edged with the rasp of their spurs. As they retraced their way through the empty rooms, a daring thought came into Mark's mind. He was convinced by now that Ann was not there. Suppose he surrendered — or better still, somehow let them get the best of him? Might they not drag him off to wherever it was Ely Timpas had gone to and so, in this way, much more swiftly bring him again into contact with Ann?

It was not the brashness of the plan that made him finally discard it; it was lack of belief in the soundness of its premise. They might kill him out of hand, or take him elsewhere — perhaps, even, merely hold him there under lock and key, safely and completely out of things. He might, on the other hand, have guessed wrong entirely. Ann may never have been there. Shain and Wilkes may have seized the girl for some dark end of their own, one utterly unrelated in any fashion to Ely Timpas. Or someone else may have grabbed her; though he thought this last unlikely.

He recalled then what Bella Mae had told him about the hills being full of riders hunting his scalp for the reward it would bring — for the bounty money being offered by Timpas.

He followed the yellow-haired man to the door.

They came onto the porch, and Conni-fay's eyes, going across the man's shoulder, went over the yard with a widening sharpness. Three still men filled the stable doorway. Two others, with rifles, were behind the corral. There was a sixth fellow flanking the saddle shed wall and, over yonder, across the baked parade of the yard, two more hired guns lounged obliquely watching him.

Connifay, with a sudden sure knowledge, understood now why they had let him come in. They had wanted to make sure of him. This was the old, old story, and danger's smell was a quickening odor while the vibrant quiet stretched thinner and thinner with the violence stored to this one grim purpose.

Somebody yelled: "Buff! Git away from that doorway!"

Said Connifay drily: "Stand still or I'll drill you," and watched sweat break across the man's cheeks.

He sent his glance round the yard again. He smiled then, coldly, and coldly waited. This was the pattern, the threadbare story so many times varied yet never quite changed. The quick death formula that men called "shoot-out" or "payoff" or "showdown" as it pleased them; a pattern which Mark, too well and too young, had learned years ago in the smoke of Smith's

Crossing. It was this which Bannock in his confident fashion had too soon called "the Last of Mark Connifay."

But these men weren't misreading their hands. They knew this would cost them something. They had counted that cost and, if they had to, would pay it. They were here to get him. They were ready. Timpas, at last, had out-figured him.

He was trapped.

The silence tightened, became insupportable. Across the way a man's shoulders lifted and Connifay pulled a deep breath through flared nostrils. The man beside him was a dead man and knew it. His face had gone completely gray.

Willow Creek Wally came out of the bunkhouse. A jubilant gloating filled his shallow eyes. He crossed the yard at a saddle-cramped swagger. A wanton lock of his rust-colored hair dangled rakishly across the baked tan of his forehead and he stopped, a cant rope's length off, to cut it away from his eyes and spit. He stood there then with his arms akimbo, a grin pulling the thin lips back from his teeth, the glint of his eyes getting surer and surer.

"You cut it a little short this time."

"So the cur makes out to be a big dog now."

Connifay's words held crystal clarity. Willow Creek's cheeks went fiery red and the flexing fingers of his dropped hand spraddled.

Somebody off to the left called urgently: *"Connifay!"*

But Willow Creek's eyes were like holes in a blanket and Connifay's glance, pure black through the crease of his lids, never wavered. He saw the lifting wink of Willow Creek's gun, saw the gleam of the sun on its blurring barrel, saw the hammer go back — and hurled himself sideways, hard into the yellow-haired man on his left. Gun sound beat at his ears like a hammer and flame was a swerving streak leaping from Willow Creek when he fired from his thigh through the bottom of his holster. The tag-end of his glance showed the yellow-haired man with recovered balance reaching a left hand outward to grab him. He shied clear of that, but the gun in the man's other fist clubbed out and the flash of it came too late to warn him. Struck across the face, he fell backward, half blinded, both arms flung out to catch at the door frame. He felt the gun torn out of his grasp. The yellow-haired Buff slammed terrifically into him, smashing his clawed fingers free of the door frame. The back of his skull struck the floor boards. His brain roared and a burst of lights exploded in his head.

Sight was a red mist that told him nothing and strength was a flood that was leaking out of him like meal from a sack with a rip in its bottom. A hazy shape came through the red fog and he knew he was done for if he didn't get up. He knew he was done for anyhow, but it wasn't in Mark Connifay to quit and, somehow, he got a wabbly knee under him. He was that way, swaying, with the hazy shape crouched blackly over him, when a boot struck his foot and the shape came down on him, smothering, solidly, bowling him over and pinning him under it.

It settled there, stayed there. He could not get loose of it. It did not fight him, it just lay on him like a chopped-down tree or the side of a house. He could hardly breathe and the pain in his head was purest agony and all the life was being squeezed out of him. He called on the last reserves of his strength and his head came free of the limp thing on him and he hauled a great breath into his lungs.

The red fog rolled away from his eyes. The dim things about him began to take shape and other sounds came through the roaring in his head — the drone of bees, he guessed they must be swarming, and an odd kind of popping like paper bags bursting. And then realization came back to him and he knew the sounds for what they were, the whine and slap of rifle lead round him; and his turning head looked into a face. It was the face of Buff and Buff was dead. Mark knew then what the weight on him was. It was Buff's dead body.

He wriggled from under it and kept on wriggling till he came to a break in the flanking wall, and all that while the whine and slap of tunneling lead kept ripping up splinters from the hallway floor boards, spattered dust and grit from the walls. The break in the wall was the living-room doorway. Mark crawled through it and pulled himself upright.

The rifle sound had quit its racket and a kind of troubled quiet settled. Connifay moved away from the wall, his breathing more regular now, and heard men's voices crossing the yard with questions. By the talk it was plain they believed they had finished him, but no one was offering to come and find out.

He did not know if his shots had put Willow Creek out of action, but he caught no word in the man's E-string growl. One thing Mark was sure of: it had been slugs from those posted leather slappers which had cut down the yellow-haired Buff. And this, he mused with a tight little smile, was commentary aplenty as to just how badly that crowd out there wanted him. Looked as if Ely's offered bounty must be a pretty sizeable one.

If he had a rifle now . . .

It was no kind of use thinking thoughts like that when all he had was a .44 pistol. He got the short-barreled gun from his shirt and wondered what had happened to his belt gun. He ought to learn what those fellows were up to. But to look would be to invite more lead, to heighten their vigilance — perhaps start something drastic.

But he'd better look, he decided finally; and on all fours he crossed to the one of the hinged windows that gave on the scene of recent action. He dragged off his hat and took a narrow view, took a thin quick breath and laid the barrel of his gun across the heavy sill.

"Just freeze right there. Both of you boys."

The taller man had a foot forward lifted; he was facing the porch and he stayed that way. But the other man, a swarthy-faced 'breed, had been eyeing the window. There was a gun in his hand and he suddenly used it, the shot knocking splinters from the frame by Mark's head.

Mark's head didn't move, but his pistol's butt kicked the palm of his hand and the 'breed's crouched shape rose three inches higher before it dropped like a too ripe apple.

The tall man stood with his eyes full of terror.

Connifay drawled: "If I have to shoot *you* it won't be through the chest. Get over here an' get here quick."

The tall man came at once, and came carefully. The fright in his eyes was almost ludicrous; and when Mark said: "I want your back up against this sill," the man put it there, without argument, hastily.

Connifay lifted the man's gun from its leather; took a quick, raking glance at the yard and leaned back.

The quiet out there was strained, was unnatural. It was not like that kind of a crew to sit coolly back and let him cut this. They were cooking up something — were bound to be.

He wished he could see them. He probed the tall man's back with his pistol while his free hand picked up his hat, put it on again. "What are them playmates of yours doin'?" he asked.

He learned before the man could open his mouth.

19. Farewell to Hope

Boots struck the porch and poured their avalanche of sound down the hallway. Connifay, whirling, was spattered with dirt from the bullet-gouged wall. Shoulders tipped, he crouched forward and with bared teeth hammered his lead at the shapes in the doorway. Powder-smoke wreathed him, blue, gyrating. A man climbing through a window across the room dropped suddenly backward with a shouted oath.

The door was vomiting flame again and Mark knew he dared not wait any longer.

He went through the window in one mad scramble, struck on his shoulder and rolled three times with the dirt spouting up like rain-struck water before he could check the rush of momentum. He came up then on two hands and a knee, got the knee wedged under him and lunged erect, making off instantly for the pole corral.

But it was no use. He knew before he'd gone ten paces it was asking too much to hope he'd make it. It wasn't in the cards for them to miss him forever. A shouted voice lifted out of the house: "Don't let the son git t' that horse!"

Boots hit the porch again and three-four rifles added their anvil notes to the bedlam, their flat *crack! crack!* cutting sharply through the lesser din of oaths and pistol racket.

There was lifted dust in the wind's lazy swirlings, dust and grit and faint streaks of gunsmoke; and the sun beat up a furnace-like heat that shimmered like water above the bright ground, and all about the blur of his boots its hoof-packed surface was scared and furrowed with the spat and whine of Wet Moon lead.

But he would not quit. His jaw was locked with a stubborn tenacity and he ran low-crouched above his pistoning knees, quartering the yard in erratic weavings that were bringing him ever nearer his horse. He could see the brute stamping and snorting nervously where he'd left him standing on ground-hitched reins. He was just beyond the bulge of the poles, less than twenty yards off, when muzzle-fire jumped from the gloom of the stable and two shots whined through the crown of his hat. A third slug tugged his vest like a hand, and a fourth creased the back of a boot, nearly pitching him.

Anger raised its white-hot hate in him, turning him bitter and uncaringly reckless, slashing the cables of judgment and caution. He spun in his tracks with pistol lifted and emptied its cylinder into the stable, searching its shadows for the riflemen hidden there and hearing, vindictively, one man's choked cry grow thin until lost in the resumed staccato pounding of the yard's lifted rifles.

He whirled to plunge on them, fumbling fresh loads from his belt for the six-gun. He felt like a man suddenly hemmed in by mad hornets. A vision of Ann rose up in his mind with its urgent reminder of why he had come there; of why — God willing — he must get out of there also. Then something hit him like an axe in the hip and the yard reeled round in a crazy blurred circle like the shaken glass in a child's kaleidoscope; and the baked adobe of the ground suddenly jumped for him, catching his chin, filling his mouth with its broken grit, slamming the shock of its impact clear down to his toe joints.

But there was no pain in him — no *real* pain, that is. Just shock, and a battered kind of numbness that was prowling over his left leg and side near his hip. The ground lay upright against his face, and all about he could see slugs slapping the grit from its hardpan. There seemed to be a kind of rumble in it too that the punch of those bullets had nothing to do with, and the spurts of dust were dancing farther away and the Wet Moon's shouts, the bang! bang! of its gunfire, seemed to be filtered by immeasurable distance.

Perhaps they were scared he was 'possuming again and were scuttling away to some safer hiding place. The thought tickled him, kind of, but he couldn't laugh because his lips were numb, were stiff and unwieldy, and his mouth tasted salty, kind of bloody-like, somehow.

Fainter and fainter grew the yard's sundry noises. The warm ground soothed him, comforting the aches and the weariness; and a feeling of peace such as he'd always longed for came like a gentle wind curling round him, making him think of the good feather bed that he'd had as a boy back home at Smith's Crossing. He'd been fond in those days of the creature comforts, he remembered amusedly; and lost the thought as he heard the closer rumble of that same ground sound which all this while had been hinting with foolish insistence that he ought to be up and about his chores.

But there weren't any chores — or were there?

He commanded himself to turn his head; and when it got turned his eyes swore he was dreaming. He halfway believed them. Every place he looked there were legs coming toward him — booted feet oddly lifting and lowering as if they were stepping on eggs and didn't want to break any.

His brain, alarmed, told his body to get out of there.

He made the effort — got an arm braced under him. The baked yard suddenly seemed to bubble up under him; to be spitting grit at him and —

He heard the shots then, the oaths and wild shouting; heard one man's voice cleaving through all the other sounds: "Damn' if the bugger ain't movin' ag'in!" and the bees got to buzzing as if he'd kicked their damn hive over; only he knew mighty well what that buzzing was now. Knew where he was, too — knew this was Wet Moon. They thought they had got him and had quit wasting lead on him. But they were at it again now, bent on sieving him proper, and he guessed they had about come close enough to do it.

A slug grazed his arm like the tail of a scorpion. It lost him his balance, but he got up anyway, and set off corral-ward with lurching, plunging steps that were awkward because he hadn't much control of that wabbly left leg. It would take his weight briefly, and that was about all. But it might do the trick — he might cheat them yet if he could get to that horse.

And it looked as if he might even do it!

He was eight yards away when the Fiddle-Back bronc the old man had lent him went up on his hind legs, screaming like a woman. Up, straight up, till its long tawny barrel was stretched like a lass rope, and you could see the rifle lead pounding its belly.

As the horse toppled backwards two men with raised Spencers sprang out of the dust of the corral and came charging.

Mark Connifay stopped dead still in his tracks.

This was the end. . . .

20. "You Don't Want Me, Do You?"

Connifay, for a man brought at last to the end of hope, did a queer thing then. With his empty hands hanging loose at his sides, he looked at the men rushing toward him and smiled — smiled with the blood dripping off his lips, and saw their stride falter, saw them pull up and stop. Something quick and surprised ran through their stares, and Connifay, hearing the thump of boots back of him, said: "Sure you want it this way, boys? Better wait for your friends. You might feel a lot safer."

With a curse the nearest man hauled up his rifle. Connifay saw the stock slap his cheek, saw the barrel steady; and flung himself forward as flame gushed out of it. He could feel the breath of the charge rip over him. With his hundred and sixty pounds of weight he hit the man just above the knees. The battering force of it hurled the man backwards. The rowels of his spurs hooked into the ground and he struck, without movement, spread-eagled on his back. The grotesque shadow of the other man sprang with clubbed rifle, and Connifay, seeing the flash of that shape, dropped at once, tripping the man with his low-crouched body. The shock of impact bowled Mark over, but the tripped man struck on his face and chin and slid out of sight in the swirling dust. Mark caught up a rifle and leaped for his horse, flattening back of it as a roaring blast from the charging crew filtered the air with its hornet humming.

He heard a shriek lift in a rising crescendo and guessed that a slug had tagged one of the pair he had just got loose of. He hoped so; and laid the captured rifle across the dead horse and triggered till the hammer hit the first spent shell. The cursing crew turned tail in a hurry and scuttled like rabbits for the nearest cover, leaving the luckless ones where they had fallen — all but the last who crawled after them doggedly.

Mark let him go, turning powder-bleared eyes toward the pole corral. He blinked and cursed and suddenly hauled himself up and, bent double, went lurching for its opened gate and the one lone horse that hadn't yet bolted.

It was tied, and its pulling and pawing had mighty nearly choked it. Mighty nearly, but not quite. It broke loose and whirled just as he got within reach of it. With a groan Mark lunged, and one outflung hand caught the flying reins and the other hand, letting go of the rifle, got a sliding grip in the roan's tangled mane.

A split second later he was on its back and spurring it madly through the ranch yard gate.

The bullet that had knocked Mark flat in the yard had not, by a miracle, lodged in his body. It was his head that was mostly bothering him, where Buff had clubbed him with the barrel of his six-shooter. To be sure, his hip felt as if a mule had kicked him, and examination had proved it blue and swollen. It was getting stiff and it made him limp when he got off the horse for anything, but the bullet hadn't even touched him; he had had the buckle of his shell belt strapped there and the broad-surfaced metal had turned the shot. The burn on his arm was more of a nuisance. But it was his battered head that was raising hob. Only his need for beating that trap had kept him on his feet and going. Danger had screwed his nerves wire taut and now they were loosening, flapping and jangling, and there were times while he rode when a gust of strong wind might easily have blown him out of the saddle.

He kept getting dizzy and the motion of the horse threatened to make him retch his guts out. He had got off the trail three-four times already and his face felt on fire and it seemed as if all the blood that he'd got left in him was trying to stuff itself into his head. He knew Buff's whack had split it open; that had been where all the blood had come from that had stuck the front of his shirt to his hide. But the bleeding had quit a long while back. The cracked edges of skin were stiff and tight to the touch of his fingers, and the flesh round his eyes had swollen and puffed till he couldn't see very well any more, till it was a painful effort to even try to. If it wasn't for Ann. . . .

But he knew what he had to do, all right. The catclaw and cacti along the trail scratched at him just as if they'd grown there apurpose to pluck him off the horse; but he laughed at them, cursed them, and kept on riding . . . though he wasn't making much time — he could see that. The sunthrown shadows had got long and black and there was a kind of reddish glow to the westward side of things that told him the sun was sinking mighty low down.

He groaned and kicked at the stumbling horse. Got to do better'n this — got to find Ann Kroniac. *Ann* — that was it! Got to find her 'fore that hog Timpas gets her. . . .

It was dark when Connifay came back to memory — to the feel of cool hands and wet cloth going soothingly over the fire of his head. Dark and chill with a risen wind blowing cold through the juniper. He thought at first that he must be dreaming, that no hands could be so soft and comforting as the light, cool touch of those moving over him. But they *were* hands — girl's hands; she had his head on her lap and he could feel her soft breath as she bent over him, working.

It was then that memory and alarm returned. "Ann —" His tongue was so thick he could hardly move it. "Ann —"

"Hush. You are hurt, I think you must have been kicked by —"

He did not wait for the last of her words. He struggled loose of the hands that would have held him, pulled free of her and came unsteadily onto his feet where he stood a bit, swaying, trying —

"You're out of your head, Mark; sit down

— sit down!" she cried, leaping up and reaching for him. "You've —"

"Never mind. Keep away. Damnation, girl, I ain't such a wreck I can't stand up!"

It wasn't, he saw, nearly as dark as he'd thought it was. But it was night, sure enough. His sight was beginning to clear a little and the patches of moonlight had quit their spinning. They were in some kind of a tiny clearing and there was something he wanted to ask Bella Mae if his head — But of course! He put a hand to his head as though he would steady it. "Where are we? — How long have I been here?"

"How can I tell how long you've been here? I found you crawlin' on the trail back there — your horse was lookin' like he thought you was crazy. Mebbe you was. You sure talkin' crazy. 'Ann! Ann! Ann!' Don't you think of nothin' but —"

"Never mind that. Where are we?"

"What are you doin' with a Wet Moon horse?" She said hastily: "All right, I'll tell you. This is Hidden Spring — we're up on Roblero. Now sit down here an' let me — Mark!" Her startled voice was almost a wail. "*Mark!* Where are you goin' — ?"

"I'm goin' to find Ann, if God'll give me the strength to."

221

He was stumbling across the gloom toward his horse where she'd left it on the grounded reins by her own, cropping the grass at the edge of the trail, when she caught him, stopping him by the surprise of her fierceness.

"Mark — you can't! Ain't you had enough of that Kroniac pride?"

"I've had enough of your lies," he said in a steel-cold way that made her look at him sharply. "Enough and to spare. Now let go of my arm —"

"Mark!"

Her upturned face was palest ivory. The moon showed him that; showed the widened eyes, the flare of her nostrils. He could not tell whether it were hurt or anger that had pulled her up so stiff and tense-like; but, suddenly, her hands were trembling. Their grip shook his arm and she was saying resentfully: "Must you always —"

"I told you. I've got to hunt Ann."

"Ann! Don't you ever think of —"

"Think! God's blood! You said yourself Ely Timpas —"

"I lied — I admit it. I was —"

"You admit it too easy," he said, disengaging her grip of his arm. "It's no use, Bella."

Her regard was strange. Even in the moonlight he could not make it out. "What's no use, Mark?" Her voice seemed thinly remote and faded as though the words came from far away. "What's no use?"

He didn't rightly know how to answer that. He said finally, bluntly: "What you been hopin' about you an' me. It won't work."

"Why won't it work, Mark?"

He wished she would talk up loud and not whisper.

"It won't work," he said, "because . . . because —"

"Because it's Ann you're wantin'? Because you don't want me — is that it?"

He looked away from the spell of her eyes. "I want you to believe, Bella, that I'd give 'most anything if . . . if things was different between us." That, at least, was God's own truth.

She said: "But you don't want me, do you, Mark?"

Perhaps if he hadn't been feeling so rotten he'd not have said the harsh thing he did then. But he did feel rotten; his head felt like a church bell banging, and all this talk wasn't helping it any.

"No!" he said, impatiently and finally.

She went back from him as though he

had struck her. Her eyes went suddenly and purely black, and she whirled to her horse and slammed into the saddle. She faced him then. "I can tell you this — *you'll never get her!*"

She was gone before her meaning reached him.

21. Reason Crawls Away

Angered, confused and queerly filled with foreboding, Connifay stared at the vibrant branches still swishing behind her tempestuous passage. Too late he was realizing the folly of frankness bluntly applied to a girl of her background. She was a cup filled to brimming with life and passion, with hunger and fire and a baleful pride that could flare to unguessed heights of spleen when flouted as it had just now been by the obvious truth of his impatient answer.

Long after the sound of her departure had dimmed away in the wooded distance, Mark Connifay stood where her words had left him, confounded and bitter, too uncomfortably aware of the unmentioned likelihoods of her tone had threatened. She might — probably *did* — know where Ann was, and . . .

He stiffened to a sudden and startling knowledge. *He was in love with Ann;* in love — God save the mark! — with a girl whose personal reaction to him was one of repugnance, extreme and scathing.

He stood irrelevantly recalling things too long forgotten in the rush of events. It seemed well nigh incredible that he, who had always drawn great pride and comfort from his will's proved mastery over basic urges, should at last have succumbed to the very urge he had foresworn strongest. No woman — he had always said — should have any part in the lot of a man gun-hounded from pillar to post.

What a consummate ass life made of him! In love with a girl who had used a quirt on him, who had openly scorned and disdained and loathed him, whose final toleration of him was but the reflection of her father's need!

Thank heaven no one need ever know it!

He lurched, still scowling, to the Wet Moon horse and pulled himself up into the saddle. He would save her if he could, and then . . .

He was too disturbed to carry the thought further, too excited and shaken by this unwonted knowledge an ironic fate had vouchsafed him at a time when he had need of all his wits to stay alive and out-guess Timpas.

He forced his thoughts to Bella Mae. Whatever the girl had done for him while he lay unconscious in this glade, she had cleared his sight considerably, anyway. He still felt like the wrath of God, but his head did not feel quite so much like a bellows, and the torn and puffed flesh above his eyes seemed not so swelled as it had been. If he remembered to sit just so in the saddle he might yet last to defeat smart Ely. He would if he could though they killed him for it.

Convinced that Bella Mae knew where they were holding Ann Kroniac captive, he was determined to follow her trail. But he found it mean work in the uncertain moonlight. Many times he was forced to get down and scan the way on hands and knees; yet false dawn found him eyeing the relic of what once had been a stout log cabin. The chinking looked pretty well crumbled now and the roof was all whoppy-jawed, warped by the elements. But Bella Mae's horse stood nearby, incurious; weary and dusty and flecked with dried lather. He could hear Bella's voice in lifted cadence coming out of the cabin, complaining and angry, and a man's curt tones said: "I'll take care of it. Do what you're told an' don't give me no sass about it."

Connifay turned, led his horse back into the timber and tied it. Then he crept again to the tree-fringed clearing and, squatting in the dew-damp undergrowth, long and gloomily considered the cabin. The voices had lowered to a mumbled monotone and he dared go no nearer without definite purpose.

There were horses in a pole corral and saddles heaped on the ground this side of it. But none of the broncs was from Ann's team. There was nothing at all to prove she was round there. This might, he thought, be the Brady cabin. The man inside might be old man Brady. There was not much sense in risking entrance without being sure they had Ann in there.

If he had a gun or some kind of weapon . . .

But he hadn't. He had no idea when he'd lost them or where, but his holsters were empty and he had no rifle. All he had was his bruised bare hands.

The only thing he could think to do was to stay where he was and keep his eye on the cabin till he knew for certain if Ann were in there.

He must have dozed.

The sun was up. There was gray smoke curling from the cabin's chimney. And the door was open, propped wide with the barrel of somebody's rifle.

Breakfast smells reached across the clearing, immeasurably adding to Mark's discomfort; adding hunger to the curse of torturing memory, to the despair and weakness that had bowed his shoulders. There was no point in fooling himself. He was bitterly aware he was not the man he had been. Fatigue and his wounds had taken their toll. His head did not feel right yet by considerable, and dizziness might overwhelm him any time. But worst of all he had no weapons — not even a skinning knife.

But if Ann were in there . . .

Impatience tugged at the set of his shoulders. If he were farther back now, say off to the right on that rise or that out-cropping, there was a smallish chance that he might be able to see into the cabin. The way the sun was streaming into that door-way, it seemed there ought to be sufficient light to determine if Ann were tied up in there somewhere.

Then, just as he was getting his lame leg under him, he saw her. She had come to the doorway and was paused in it with the sun's light bright in the piled-up braids of her tawny hair. Yet even at that distance — a good twenty yards — he could see how drawn and blanched were her cheeks, could see the dark smudges underneath her eyes. He strained with the breath hung up in his throat as he saw the shudder that involuntarily shook her.

He groaned at the hopeless look of her then, understanding what nightmare she must have been through since two nights ago when he'd left her in the wagon before the Cap and Ball. He could well guess, too, what prospect was hers after the vile hints she must have had from her captors.

Abruptly he noticed how her shape had straightened, had gone still and tense. He went taut himself when he saw where she looked, too well understanding the long-odds chance that was in her mind. She was eyeing those horses in the pole enclosure. Bella Mae's saddled pony was no longer in sight; she must have turned it in with the others.

Ann's lips had hardened. She had made up her mind.

She was going to chance it.

A gabble of talk had broken out in the cabin. Bella Mae's talk, with Brady's voice breaking through it, ordering Ann back away from the doorway. Bella Mae's laugh sheared the air, scornful and quick, and a chair creaked loudly as someone lunged up. Brady's loud bellow cried, "By —" and cut viciously short as Ann dashed from the cabin.

Connifay, desperately attempting to count the heaped saddles, swung with a smothered oath when the scuff of Ann's boots hit the shaley path. A forlorn admiration showed its glint in his eyes as he watched the sun-brightened gleam of her boots as her sprinting stride took her nearer and nearer the rickety rails of the pole enclosure. If he'd only had some kind of a gun —

She was barely ten feet from the corral's fastened gate when a stone turned under her and pitched her sprawling.

A groan squeezed out of Connifay's throat.

She was up in an instant but the chance was gone. Brady, plunging from the cabin, flung up his rifle. Ann, head turned, saw him over her shoulder. Hope and courage died hard on her features. She seemed to shrink as she stood there, her slim shape twisted in the maze of trapped emotion, her mouth half opened in a wail pride would not let her loose. Her eyes went dull as hope walked out of them and her head tipped forward, acknowledging defeat.

Brady did not leer, not then. He was too bull mad with the thought of what she might have done. The tufts of hair on the backs of his fingers stood out jet black against the grip of his rage. "Yuh git back in here! An' come a-humpin' 'fore I —"

"Hold it, Brady!"

A new voice, that. Not a loud voice. An odd, kind of choked, low voice thick with a terrible, deadly earnestness. It stopped Brady's talk like a hand on his shoulder.

Ann's head came up and her lifted eyes had a new, wild light in them. She knew that voice.

It seemed Brady knew it, too. The red heat of anger drained from his face, leaving it skimmed and blue like milk with the cream off. And his eyes showed still, still and fixed as if someone had blown cold air down his neck; and the black hairs were prickling on his bare, burly forearms, standing stiff like the hairs sticking out of his ears. His tongue looked as if it, too, were stiff as it edged through his cracked, suddenly colorless lips as though it would wet them into speaking shape. They did move finally, but no words came.

The voice said: "Throw that rifle over here in the bushes."

Bella Mae stepped down from the doorway and stood just behind the froze shape of the hillman. She touched his arm.

The jerk of her head swung her red curls eastward. "Over there," she said, her painted cheeks expressionless. "Just this side of that limestone shoulder. He's in the brush alongside of that pinion."

Brady's tongue was working better. It licked his lips. His head came slowly round to look, and the cotton shirt stretched tight across his chest as the muscles of his bony shoulders leaped the rifle up; but the girl was too quick for him. She knocked the barrel up. Flash and report threw their charge at the tree tops.

"You cravin' to get planted? Do like he says," Bella Mae shrilled fiercely. "Throw that saddle gun over there! It's that gamblin' man, Connifay! Just as lief kill you as bash your face for you! *You* ought to know that! Do like he tells you!"

Cheeks twisted by the clutch of his passions, Brady did as bidden, but his eyes were wicked.

"Get away from him, Bella," the voice said. "My aim —"

Like the strike of a snake Brady's arm curled out, closed round the girl's waist and yanked her against him. A pistol jumped from his belt, spitting flame.

Bella fought the grip of that clamping arm, kicked at his shins, threw her weight every which way, but his shots kept ripping the brush by the pinion like hailstones pounding the cloth of a tent wall.

When the gun was shot dry, Connifay's voice, thick with rage, growled: "Ann! Get on a horse an' get out of here."

Temptation and terror seemed to fight for Ann's will, but she shook her head stubbornly. "Not till you go. I won't —"

Connifay's harsh tones slashed at her bitterly. "For once in your life, girl, do like you're told! Don't stand there an' argue! Grab a horse an' get outa here!"

The pink of her cheeks showed the sting of his words. But she held her ground, not budging a step, while her worried eyes searched the undergrowth for him.

Bella Mae's eyes were searching the brush, too; but she moved quickly enough when her father let go of her. She went floundering into it, headed dead south; but they'd all caught the hoof sound before she'd obscured it.

Connifay's voice cracked sharp as a whiplash. "Ann! Get out of here!"

She wavered, irresolute, her mobile cheeks suddenly blanched of color. "But *you!*" The words were an anguished cry and she had started toward him, a desperate pleading in her eyes.

"In God's name, get back — *get back!*" Mark cried. "You heard them horses! Get out of here —" His voice broke harshly. *"Just one more move, Mister Brady, an' they'll be takin' your size for a coffin."*

But there was no fear now on the gun-runner's cheeks. Derision shaped the quirk of his mouth. All the lines of his face had altered and a jubilant impudence leered from his stare. He cuffed back the brim of his hat and spat, and a hard grin peeled his lips off his teeth. "Yo're slick, by Gawd — I give yuh credit! But yuh ain't foolin' Joe Brady none. Not any, yuh ain't! If yuh'd had any gun, by grab, yuh'd of used it!"

His head tipped back in a raucous laugh. "I'll settle yo' —"

His fleeting glance caught a blur that whirled him around. He stared and swore. Tumultuous anger unsettled his voice and his blatted yell slammed across the clearing like hot lead thrown from his heaved-away rifle. *"Git off'n that hawse, yuh brazen scut! I'll fetch yo' —"*

"Keep goin'! Keep goin'!" Mark shouted hoarsely, and breasted the clutch of the brush like a steer, oblivious to thorns, head down in a rush for Brady's rifle.

It was over there somewhere in that rank growth of nettles that carpeted the ground all about the gnarled pinion. He saw the butt sticking out of a catclaw — saw Brady whirling to snatch for the rifle that was holding the cabin door propped open. He put every ounce of speed he could muster in a hurtling dive at the catclaw thicket. One thorn-ripped hand closed round the stock. His scratched head throbbed to the hammer of hoofs as he jerked up onto one knee with the gun.

Brady had gotten the other rifle, and the look of him as he brought it up showed he meant to shoot either Ann or the horse.

Connifay prayed for the first time in years as he levered a cartridge up into the barrel. He brought the butt up against his shoulder. The light was bad; it was dead against him, a glint on the barrel, a fuzzy kind of halo round the head. But he had no time to better it. The horsemen he'd heard to the south, by the sound, were no more than yards from the edge of the clearing.

He hunted for something on Brady to aim at, caught the flash of the concho securing the ends of the gun-runner's hat straps, and fired, while Brady's own report jarred into the echoes.

He saw the smash of his lead take Brady, saw the blood gush out of his mangled face. . . .

With his insides heaving, he saw Shain and Wilkes burst out of the brush. He emptied the rifle as they flung themselves frantically out of their saddles. Shain — it looked as if he'd missed Vidal Shain completely; but he could hear Wilkes thrashing in the brush by the trail side.

The clearing was going round and he knew by the cramps in his lungs he was retching; but he dared not wait till the dizziness passed. He must find that Wet Moon horse he'd left tied — find it and go before he got himself trapped there.

It was dusk and a ground wind was rolling up behind him as he topped the last rise that lay between him and the Fiddle-Back. He was just about used up. His eyes felt like holes burned in a blanket and his insides — it didn't rightly seem as if he had any nowadays; he hoped they were keeping some grub on the stove for him . . . grub, and a bunk he could pound his ear in.

He'd thought about Ann a great deal during the ride, what time he wasn't either dozing or dizzy; and he'd made another, an astounding discovery. Back there at Brady's Ann had been afraid for him — *afraid* for *him!* There was no getting round it. She'd been beside herself. Under their tan her cheeks had been bloodless and, scoff as he had at such a preposterous concept, he could not forget what he'd seen in her eyes.

What would she say to him, now that she was home again and safe with her father? Not that *he'd* ever open the subject. There were two or three things even a tinhorn could savvy. But he guessed she'd never be hurt by his thinking of how things *might* have been if *she* hadn't been fetched up so proud and *he* hadn't been a gambling man. . . .

His eyes went suddenly black and wide.

He realized finally that the horse had stopped. That the horse had been stopped a long, long time. That his throat was so dry he couldn't swallow — that dust had got into the staring eyes he had fixed on the place where the Fiddle-Back had stood.

Had stood was right.

It was not there now. There was nothing there now but the burnt-out ashes of gutted buildings that would never throw back Ann's laugh again.

22. Jornada

It took all Mark's waning energy to keep from spurring his horse down the trail. But he forced himself to take it slow, to allow himself time for readjustment. He had put the first ugly panic down; he could not know anything, could form no right opinions or arrive at conclusions that held any soundness, until he had fingered, had sifted those ashes.

The hollow *whoom* of the little plank bridge was a dismal sound as the horse walked across it, but it wasn't one tenth as forlornly dreary as the prospect churning the fog of his thoughts.

But conclusions came, whether sound or not; and it was a hard, bitter man, burning-eyed, filled with hate, who finally half fell off the horse to stumble across the remains of the porch and view what was left of the Kroniac ranch house.

He did not finger the ashes though, nor sift them, nor prowl through the yard to cut sign of the things that had happened there. He had no need. A gangling shape that he remembered well stepped catlike from the wreck of the chimney with a six-gun swiveled in a ready fist.

"So you're back."

"Didn't you reckon I would be? Where's Ann? Ain't you seen her? Where's the Ol' Man? Where's Tony? When did Timpas' crowd —"

"You always was a hell-tearer f' questions." Silver Dollar came with his graveled tones round the burnt-down stump of a porch post and stood with his cat's eyes cocked and calculating. His cud-bulged cheek hugged a tight kind of grin. "Your mug looks like a pack horse kicked it —"

"Never mind my mug. I pried Ann loose an' had her headin' —"

"You needn't worry 'bout Ann. There's a new deal opened an' *I'm* roddin' things now." The spread-apart lips of Ann's uncle tightened. "I'm callin' the tune an' you can dance or . . ." His flourished pistol suggested the alternative. "The Ol' Man's dead — got wiped out in the raid. Tony's off some place he allowed to know about, huntin' his sister —"

"I'm surprised you ain't. Don't your niece's safety —"

Silver cut in smoothly: "I been waitin' for you. Had a hunch you'd be back. You can forget about Ann. Bella Mae'll take care of her —"

"Bella Mae, eh?" Connifay leaned on his rifle. A cold distrust looked out of his stare. "So Bella Mae'll take care of her. Don't you know Bella Mae is workin' with Timpas?"

"The point," Silver grinned, "is who *you're* workin' with."

Something was plain enough to Connifay then. He lifted his bone-tired weight off the rifle with turbulent awareness making him savage. "So you're that breed of cur! You've sold out to Timpas, have you? I always knew you for a crook, but I didn't suppose even *you* would be hound-low enough to see your own flesh an' blood —"

"That's enough o' that guff!" Silver Dollar's cheeks were a fiery red. "*I* didn't leave her in front of that saloon! It was *you* had to go an' make things easy for 'em! As for Timpas — you're right; of course I'm backin' him! Do I look like a *fool?*"

He glared at Connifay a long, still moment. Then he spoke placatingly. "Nothin's going to happen to her, long's she uses her head a little. Ely's willin' to marry her yet — even willin' to forget you was in Mesilla with her. He's a fair-minded man.

241

But you got to admit he don't need her no more. Kroniac's dead, an' prob'ly Tony — if he ain't he will be. The fightin's all over. What's left of these two-bit, flip-flap outfit's'll do mighty quick what Ely tells 'em to."

He smiled expansively, gesturing with his pistol.

"We don't need you, Mark — we got this thing all licked. Timpas can call this country his clean north ten miles above the Elephant Buttes. But there's the matter of a little rep I've give you; might just be we could find some use for it. Anyhow," he grinned, "if you want to come in . . ."

"I think," Mark said, deceptively quiet, "there's a name in the Bible that fits you, Silver."

A dull flash spread across the sheriff's face and his eyes flashed black as the soul inside him. "You tinhorn fool!"

White flame leaped out of the gun in his fist, but the shot was fired by a finger's reflex. He was a dead man, reeling, when his pistol spoke.

It was dark when Connifay found the man's horse.

There was food in the saddlebags and he wolfed it cold. Afterwards, hobbling the horse so it shouldn't get away, he rolled up in Silver's blankets.

His head had come off the saddle — was on the ground with all the lines of his face relaxed, when the rifle's report slammed its challenge through the tumbled slopes of the Organ foothills.

Mark's grounded face stayed flat where it was, but he was instantly and fully, very vigilantly, awake, with his cocked ears probing the night for knowledge. He had made no fire and he thanked the Lord he hadn't. There was nothing but the dim and very nearly down moon to give searching eyes any key to his whereabouts. Tired as he had been, sick and sore in spirit, he had not forgotten the need for care. He had made his bed in the gloom of the willows alongside the quiet of the rippleless stream.

So he wasn't seen; he was assured of that. Yet he kept his place for long, crouched moments while the last, final tumult of the sound died away.

Fog lay in the hollows now; it was damp on his hair, wetly beading his rifle where it lay on the ground within quick reach of his hand. The shot, he decided, had not been fired far away. Not farther, he thought, than the rock-rimmed draw that split a gash through the hills on the trail to Jackson's — which meant, precisely, not above two miles northeast of there.

He came up on an elbow intently, grimly, listening. And presently heard what he'd expected to hear. Another shot, much farther off — west, this time; and, two minutes later, another, from the south.

Signals.

Bella Mae had said, and quite truthfully it seemed, that Timpas had men out combing the hills for him. Shain, evidently, had reached some of them with word of what had happened at Brady's. Perhaps they knew where he was; knew, at least in general. Someone in the mountains may have caught him through a glass. It made no difference what, or how, they knew; they were spreading a circle, and the only answer to that. . . .

He pulled the gun belt with Silver's sheathed pistol from under his saddle, and threw off the blankets. He came, cat soft, to his feet and buckled the belt around him, thonging the holster down with its whang strings. Scooped up his hat and put it gingerly on while his eyes searched the fog-dappled, dark-obscured distance. Then he caught up the rifle, made sure it was loaded, snapped a couple of big branches from the nearest willow and so arranged them under the blankets as to make it seem he still lay there, sleeping.

He was glad now he'd left Silver's horse under saddle. The tall, long-legged gray looked up from its cropping to eye him curiously. Working swiftly, Connifay transferred the hobbles to the bronc he had borrowed from the Wet Moon, and led that animal out into the open where approaching riders would be sure to see it. Having done then all he could to further the deception, he swung up into the gray's damp saddle.

The sleep had done him good. His head was still sore and his muscles ached with every movement, but his mind was clear and the gash on his forehead had stopped its thumping. He must run for it now, that he might live on to fight another time. He must head northwest if he would slip past the hunters, and he must do it now before their circle closed in on him.

He dared not take to the full open yet, though he knew if he could not presently swing directly east or west, and they discovered his flight, they would force him into the desert. The desert bags hung across Silver's pommel were full and cold, but that burning stretch of sand north-westward was the last thing he cared to buck in the shape these last days had put him in. However, he had no choice for the moment. First things first — and the first thing now was to slip these bounty-hunters closing on the Fiddle-Back's gutted buildings.

He dipped into the scrub that flanked the hills and, higher, merged with the solid, unbroken black of timber. But he dropped down out of that hastily; there were riders up there, and they were working toward him, dragging the brush with a wealth of noise and shouted profanity.

He dropped down into the juniper and struck due north at a faster clip, knowing the racket above would cover for a while all sound of his progress. It was the hastening departure of night that worried him. Already the serrated eastern skyline was revealing a noticeable tinge of gray. He must either be into the hills beyond the hunters or completely away from them before day came; and he knew abruptly how far beyond hope were these alternatives. Against the brightening eastern haze he saw a dark file of riders rushing north full tilt.

Knowing the Organs closed to him, he swung the gray left, dead into the west, in the hope of making the Sierra Caballos, fervently counting that the riders over there whose signal he'd heard were long since out of them, gone into the south. He was suddenly seized by a mounting and terrible need for speed; there were fifteen miles of wasteland ahead, much of it open, before he could reach —

He pulled the gray up on its haunches, startled. There was no use trying it. When the sun came up they would spot him and have him — have him trapped between them; and the riders he had seen rushing north would turn back and block his last slim chance to get free.

He sat there, scowling, teeth worrying his lips, while his eyes searched the lanes of the thinning juniper; and the feeling of danger strengthened and grew and for the first time in his life he felt confidence leaving him. He sank spurred heels to the big gray's flanks, then, savagely cursing, pulled the horse to a stop. He was acting like a fool — like a panicky greenhorn! He must not let himself become unsettled. Swiftly, inexorably as this trap was closing, he was not caught yet. There was one way left. One way — the Jornada. He would be sighted, of course, before he ever got into it. But it was the only chance.

He eased the big horse on a downgrade course that put the last of the trees behind. Daybreak found him on the valley floor, holding the gray to an easy lope that was covering ground and yet conserving its strength for the ordeal ahead.

And it would be an ordeal. The evil fame of the Jornada del Muerto was known all across the length and breadth of this land; it was the most terrible stretch of desert known. It was desolation without respite. Mile after mile of breathless, firehot waste. Had his own fate been all he had to think of, he would never have considered tracking into that sand; but there was Ann. Her face was before him always. He dared not think what fate might be hers were she left to Timpas' tender mercies. How far, and to what purpose, the man would dare go was problematical; Mark's mind shied from even the thought of it. Next to his awareness of his feelings for Ann, hatred of Timpas had become the most consuming passion he had ever known; it was overwhelming every other emotion, desire and need. The man was an octopus, strangling the country, strangling every last thing that was clean and decent.

He had been keeping a sharp lookout, hoping to spot the bunch of riders he had seen rushing north before they should catch sight of him. He was not quite sure whether to feel glad or cheated when he came out onto the last of land without having caught any sign of them.

The last of land was the broken rim of the valley floor where it dropped, eroded and chancy, for a long, fifty feet of scooped-out slope, untracked sand of the desert itself. Seen as Connifay now saw it, in the vermilion glow of the rising sun, it was a land at once fantastic and impossible, an incredible world of sand, rock and sun, without tree or shade, waterless and lifeless, stretching illimitably beyond the reach of eye or glass to a final blending with the sky itself at some infinite point beyond the mind's conception.

It was monstrous, staggering, overwhelming in the vastness of its space and silence. But Connifay was not pausing to consider it. Other than that first startled stare, he gave it no attention, but confined his energies to seeking the least hazardous way of getting down to it. Sitting motionless in the saddle, he took one final look behind him, then urged the gray toward what appeared to be a kind of trail which, in one of the eroded channels scoring the sandstone face of the slope, eventually got him down without mishap. Though the sun was not a quarter hour up when the gray stepped trembling into the sand, the temperature must have been well above ninety; a breathless ninety that bathed Mark Connifay's back with sweat and made him unstopper the nearest waterbag. The soothing gurgle coursing down his throat was immeasurably satisfying.

He saw not a track on the undulant surface of the sand's hard crust, no marks of even an animal's claws. Forlorn and stark it stretched away like a sea that had frozen and refused to thaw out.

Despite the breathless quality of the heat they made good time in that first couple of hours. The hard packed sand was like a beach road; and then, without warning, its texture changed, became unstable and deeply yielding. The gray's hot hoofs sank in to the hocks and came out as if they had sunk in molasses. At some time past ten the desert's surface changed again and Mark found himself in a region of dull black rock, with naked black crags cutting the glare of sand like the vertebrated contours of monsters from another world. It was a nightmare country and he would be glad to be quit of it.

It was while they were stopped in the

tepid shadow of the last gaunt rib, and he was watering the gray from the crown of his hat, he saw, cutting toward him out of the shimmering east, the wavering shapes of hunched-forward horsemen. He scrubbed a hand across his sun-tortured eyes and peered again from its shaking shadow.

It was they, all right — the black file of horsemen he had seen before daylight rushing silently north ahead of him.

They were not rushing now. They were wallowing as badly as the gray had been; phantom shapes in a world gone mad, grotesque creatures awkwardly shambling toward him. Their number had dwindled — perhaps some had fallen victim to these burning wastes — but those who were left were still of a mind to fulfill their purpose.

They were not, Mark thought, over three miles off; and he cursingly dragged himself into the saddle. They had seen him. He saw, in a backward look flung across his shoulder, the leading caricature lift a pointing hand — saw the wink of metal, knew he waved a rifle; saw all six of the creatures kicking their stilt-gaited nags to an increased speed that was a floundering stagger.

But Mark's gray was floundering, too;

and the chug of its breath was a rasp, shrill and whistling. And now, of a sudden, a wind whipped up, furnace hot and fanned with death. The molten glare of the brassy sky grew overcast. A hazy dimness rose and spread, enveloping the north in a lemon fog that blotted out even the sand's fierce glare. Mark's brain teemed with the tales he had heard of unfortunates caught upon this baleful waste by just such things as that yonder pall which, shrinking and swelling and whirling dizzily, was rushing toward them at unbelievable speed.

In a frantic effort to get out of its path his spurred heels sent his heaving horse straight west in a floundering gallop. Perhaps they missed the worst of it. All Mark knew was that the world gave a sudden screech of fury and all the sand of the desert came at him, and the gray heeled round with its rump to the wind and, though both Mark's fists choked a hold on the saddle horn, the lash of the gale almost tore him loose before the terrified horse gave up and went wallowing off through the trough of the storm.

Mark had tied his neckerchief over his face, but he could scarcely breathe and the flying grit had the force of hail — of buckshot; and he forgot which way was up and which down, and he prayed that the hands he had wrapped round the horn could keep their hold so long as his mind kept hold of consciousness.

The roar of the wind grew wilder and wilder; its gusts had veered and were shrieking now from the obscured east with fierce shoves there was no resisting. He never knew when he lost the horse, but realized suddenly it was gone from under him — that he was floundering alone, reeling and stumbling, fighting to keep his feet against the lash of the wind that kept slapping and slapping and slapping him westward.

He was staggering blindly, gasping and dazed, when awareness came — filtered through the numbed hulk of him — that the wind had lulled, that the sand had quit pounding him. Reaction dropped him prone, and it was many minutes before he roused sufficiently to fumble the neckerchief off his face. The storm had passed; he could see its gray pall away off to the west and nearer, not barely over a mile away, showed the mouth of a draw.

Mark grew suddenly conscious of the intense heat. The sun once more like a baleful fire was flooding the desert with its killing light. Mark felt he should go blind from the fearful glare, and heat waves danced and shimmered weirdly, and he remembered the mirage he had seen that morning of the beautiful lake and the tall, green trees; and he began to wonder as he stumbled toward it if the yonder draw were not the same: a figment of imagination, a phantom — some ghastly deceit as unreal as the bird sounds he thought to have heard from it, an hallucination to tempt and lure him to his own destruction, filling his fevered brain with hope, yet empty as a midnight dream, retreating always, drawing back with each lurched stagger of his stumbling feet.

Yet ever and again he scrambled up to go floundering on, beguiled and bemused with his need for water, unfaltering in his blind belief that a few steps more must surely bring him to it. His tongue was swollen, parched and stiff; his cracked lips gasped — each breath a torture in the worn-out bellows of his burning lungs.

He was crawling, finally, seared eyes fixed in a red-rimmed stare that could place the draw no nearer through the shimmering, smoking curls of heat. He lost all track of time, of pain. He must have kept crawling, kept worming on, but he remembered nothing of that final lap when sense at last brought him vision again and he found himself half submerged in the shallows of a green-scummed sump.

It had not, it seemed, been a mirage after all. Sandstone walls, blood red and steep, rose on both sides of him, climbing skyward. He was in a canyon that bent, just ahead, in a sudden angle that blocked all sight. And his rearward view, at twelve hundred yards, was blocked as well by a similar bend.

He lay awhile, drawing breath from the shade of the gnarled old spruce that leaned above him, the feel of the mud cool as ruffled grass under him, soothing his shriveled and sun-baked flesh. His legs had quit hurting. His head felt better, though his eyes still stung as if he'd got soap into them, and all of his muscles felt stretched and slack.

But he got up presently, pulling himself from the water, pausing a moment to scoop up a handful and swig it into his cottony mouth, rolling it gurgling across his tongue as if he'd never before known how good it could be.

He was like that, bent, still smacking cracked lips, when a hollow clatter of steel-shod hoofs hurled its racketing echoes off the canyon walls.

Connifay stayed in the pose but was suddenly tense. His eyes came up, bright between their red rims — hard and coldly narrow as a wolf's. All the harsh realities of his presence there came flooding back to dismay and stiffen him. Thoughts of Ann — of Ann's plight, of the hell of her whereabouts and his score against Timpas, roused the dregs of his anger and thrust him erect with his turning head raking sharp stares about him. When his look swung east his jaws were locked. There was still one chance and he was going to take it.

He broke into a shambling, lurching run, heading up the trail, cursing as he fumbled the gun from Silver's buttoned holster to see the trickle of water come out of it.

He made the bend, went caroming round it and saw, just ahead, an opening where a side canyon struck off. He shook the dripping six-shooter, irritably scrubbed it on his steaming shirt while he cursed his crazy, stumbling feet that refused to land where his will directed. Still running, he shook the loads from the cylinder; there was nothing more useless than dampened powder. He remembered then the way he had lain when awareness returned to find him spraddled half in and half out of the pool and, remembering, thrust his free left hand to the back of his belt, there finding four filled loops that still were dry. He fumbled out their precious loads and crassed them into Silver's gun while loud and ever louder swelled the rattle, bang and clang of hoofs so swiftly closing the way behind.

His lurching run had brought him but a bare and stumbling hundred yards, but this was all that he could do — he could not run another step. The follies of his life rose up and stalked before the curtain of his mind; the mistakes of haste, harsh judgments made, trooped by, one by one; and clear through every picture peered the pleading, haggard face of Ann.

The knuckles of his clenched fists gleamed like moon glint on Yukon snow as he lifted up his face and cursed, the breath hard-sobbing through his teeth.

To think he should have come so far — so wearily, bitterly far, to find himself where he stood now; to the realization of a dismal truth too well, he thought, foreshadowed always. That Ann and he . . . Ann — *Ann!* Dear God — *Ann Kroniac!*

The blood was pounding through his head. It beat and throbbed Ann's name unanswerably — Ann's name and God's, between the groans that squeezed apart his heat-cracked lips while his eyes, his staring glare-glazed eyes, looked up and cursed the sandstone walls that all ringed him round, blood red and steep — full thirty feet, to trap him there and end all things as they'd begun . . . in timeless sleep.

23. "Tell Me When —"

This was it.

Connifay knew that at last he was through. Caught in this echoing trap of a canyon that had no outlet but the way he'd come, there could be no longer any room for doubt. A thread-bare axiom of the past was proved: No man could run from destiny, or leave his luck behind. The Connifay luck had caught up with him.

Had caught up with him — yes; but he wouldn't quit. It was not the Connifay way to quit. Not till the last white chip was gone. Nor then. No Connifay quit till Death closed the game.

The clatter of hoofs was just round the bend when Mark spun round and went lurching back. In this barren gulch there was not a weed for cover; he had to get as close to that bend as he could if he would glean what advantage might lie in surprise and a lessened range for his shaking hand.

He was not ten feet from it, flat to the wall, when a cursing rider came spurring round it on a windblown roan that could scarcely stagger. Mark's six-shooter bucked in his hand and the horse went down with a slug through its brain, flinging its rider headlong over it to land in a crumpled heap on the ledge rock.

It was in Mark's mind to get the man's gun, or at least some cartridges out of his shell belt; but time wouldn't let him. He was stumbling forward with that intention when hoofbeats drummed along the rim above and two men sloshed round the bend, guns lifted. Sun flashed off them, flame gouted out of them; Mark's bleary gaze went out of focus and men and horses seemed to melt together like something in water color whirled from an easel. A horse's shoulder caromed against him, driving him hard toward the canyon wall. The shock of impact reached all through him, and millions of miles away someone said: "Smash him, Deke! Blow his damn' head off!" and the red rocks seemed to sway and gibber with the churned up clamor that was boiling off them. Then abruptly he got his knees up under him and through a red fog saw a shape before him and clubbed at it with his pistol before he realized the shape was already falling.

He clawed a hold on the wall with his left arm to brace himself and shook his head to clear the sweat from his eyes — or maybe it was blood, he thought disgustedly. That was where he shone. He had a talent for blood.

He grew presently aware that the walls had quit ringing; that someone was nudging him, saying something to him. He felt weary with a fatigue that was not a need for sleep alone. "Connifay — Connifay! Snap out of it, damn it — there's work to be done!"

That was the hell of having a conscience; always after a man, always nagging. "Go 'way," he mumbled; but the talk wouldn't quit.

Seemed pretty loud for conscience, somehow. Must be one of those dead men got up to argue. By grab! It *was!* Couldn't make much sense of the fellow's face, but he'd got plenty body onto him, looked like. The body was shaking him. Mark didn't like it. "Here — drink this!"

That was carrying it pretty damn far, Mark thought. Fellow you'd just killed shouldn't be drinking with you. But he hoisted the bottle. No corpse was going to show a Connifay manners. He took a good stiff swig — took another, to prove it.

261

The gulch swung suddenly into sharp focus. "Young Kroniac, eh? Look pretty spry for a dead man, Tony." Mark shook his head, and handed back the bottle. "That's aplenty; I'm all right now. How'd you get here?"

"Came down from the rim."

Connifay looked and saw the rope. "Got a horse up there?"

"Two of them. Fetched one along for Ann —"

"Ann! You know where she's at?" Connifay's grip dug the kid's shoulder hard. He appeared suddenly, fiercely, very much alive.

"Yeah — in a cabin. Slick hideout — ain't keepin' no watch out at all, not hardly." The kid seemed older, sterner, more sensible. Even his voice was different — terse, a man's voice; as though in these troubles he had found himself.

Connifay could understand that; he had found himself, too. He said: "Let's have it."

Without wasting words Tony told how he came to be there. He had heard, some time ago, two of Timpas' gun hands talking about a hideout Timpas had near Elephant Butte. All you had to do to get there was to follow the western rim of the desert. Tony, thinking they might be holding Ann there, had followed it. He'd been watching the place all day. Shain, Bella Mae and the Currycomb boss, Hackberry, were holding Ann there pending Timpas' arrival. Timpas had just ridden in from the north. Tony, watching the place from the rimrock, had seen Mark Connifay come off the desert, had seen the men trailing him. Knowing himself powerless to effect Ann's release without help, he had come over here to give Mark a hand. If Mark could ride they had better get going.

Mark agreed. "Reckon you can haul me up that rope?"

"If I can't, I guess the horses can."

"Go on up then. I'll tie it round me." Connifay picked up his pistol and rummaged for cartridges. Timpas' gun fighters had some they wouldn't be needing. He reloaded the six-shooter and filled out the empty loops of his belt.

The sun was a low, red blaze in the sky when they sighted the cabin. It was a long, built-of-logs affair set snugly under the red rock overhang. There was a trickle of smoke curling out of its chimney and horses penned in the brush close by. Saddles were heaped alongside the doorway and there was no one in sight, though the door stood open and the mutter of voices could be plainly heard.

"Funny," Mark said, "they ain't keepin' a lookout. That firin' —"

"Couldn't hear it here. Wind was howlin' through that spruce up there. What do you reckon we better do?"

Mark said softly, "You —" and stopped, eyes narrowing. A man, Tod Hackberry, had just come out and was carrying a bucket off into the trees. Mark scanned the steep trail leading down to the cabin. "I'm goin' down there. You stick right here an' keep your rifle handy. When Hackberry comes back start makin' a distraction." He went off before young Kroniac could protest over the part he had given him.

He was almost to the cabin, working cautiously through the juniper, well over to the left so that anyone looking out the door would not be likely to see him, when Tony let go with his rifle. He heard Tod Hackberry's lone, high shout shear into a tight and brittle stillness; heard again the crash of Tony's Spencer — heard its lead ripping tunes through the cabin stovepipe.

Mark was close now, almost up to the doorway. The door was still open; no one had dared come forward to close it. He could vaguely glimpse, just inside and beyond it, a man with a rifle crouched under the window. Mark, guessing it to be Shain, was again edging forward when Timpas appeared at the door with a pistol and coolly fired four shots at the rimrock. He had ducked back again before Mark could drop him. But Shain had seen Mark — was lifting his rifle when Mark, jumping up, made a lunge for the doorway.

Tony's gun had gone silent; Mark could hear him running. And Shain, as Mark's shape crossed the threshold, dropped flat on his belly with his eyes almost popping and both shaking hands thrust empty in front of him. Mark whirled and saw he had not a second to spare. Bella Mae stood rooted just left of the doorway. Beyond her, backed against the cabin wall, was Ann. Within arm's length of Ann, reaching for his belt where it hung from a chair back, crouched Timpas, caught with only one shot in his pistol.

Even as Mark placed him, Shain came rushing off the floor. The force of his clutch wheeled Mark around. Mark struck him hard with the barrel of his six-gun and heard skirts rustle as Shain's knees folded. Mark spun and his raking glance saw Bella, back toward him and with head held high, standing square in the track of Timpas' fire.

Sweat laced the dust on Connifay's cheekbones. "Bella —"

"No!"

He tried to edge from behind her but she wouldn't let him. Timpas said: "Bella Mae, stand away from that man —"

"I'm comfortable."

"Stand aside!" Timpas shouted.

"I won't!"

"Then stay there, damn you!" Timpas' gun spat fire.

Mark stood frozen.

Tony sprang past him and caught Bella Mae, easing her gently, almost tenderly, down. He dropped to his knees, repeating her name in a choked, dry voice that was sounding the nethermost depths of despair; and Connifay, seeing how it was with him, understood with a profound pity what it was this girl had held against the Kroniacs.

And then, remembering Timpas, he was raising his gun when Ann cried: "No, Mark — *no!* Let the law take care of him —"

"The law! *What* law?" Tony's eyes lifted

sharply. They were crazed and ugly. He came full erect. "You've a gun in your hand, Timpas — *use it!*"

Mark went out to the horses with the crash of that shot still banging its racket against the logs of the cabin. Ann found him there, wearily saddling the mounts in the brush corral. She came with her stricken face and stood by him. "All this blood . . . this killing. Will there never be an end to it?"

"I think the end has been reached," Mark said. "Bella Mae once told me nothing would ever stop Timpas but death. No one else of his gang has the wit or vision —"

"Then you know?"

"What he was after? Yes. Tony told me. He dreamed he could compound the waters of the Rio Grande in the sinks up here around Elephant Butte . . . build a water reserve —"

"That was why he wanted title to all the valley lands," Ann said. "With water he could bring the railroad. He meant to sell every inch of the desert to the farm hungry fools —"

"Ann . . ." Mark said, and at once she turned and was crying softly, intensely with her golden head pressed against his shoulder.

He put his arms around her, humbly, not knowing she had conquered pride. The fragrance of her hair was close; it tricked his stumbling tongue to speech. He had to know one way or the other, and he said, his tone suddenly hungry and desperate: "Ann —"

But she shook her head. "Don't tell me, Mark — just hold me tight. Tell me after I'm wife to a gamblin' man; tell me when I'm Mrs. Mark Connifay, dear . . ."

About the Author

Nelson Nye is an author of Westerns who has been himself a rancher, cattle-puncher, and horse-breeder. He's an authority on quarter horses and used to raise them on his own ranch. He now lives in Tucson, Arizona.

One of the guiding lights of the Western Writers of America, Nelson Nye has had quite a raft of good novels published under his own signature and a few pen names as well, and is quite proud of having won the WWA Spur Award for *Long Run*, an Ace Book. He is the 1968 winner of the Golden Saddleman Award, which goes to the person who has contributed most to the field of Western Americana.